TURN ME ON

J. KENNER

M&O

Turn Me On

by

J. Kenner

About Turn Me On

Sometimes one night just isn't enough.

Though they see each other only once a month, Amanda's sweet body and wicked ways have been driving Derek wild for over a year.

And now that he's moving to Austin, Derek is determined to have Amanda in his bed permanently.

There's only one problem: Amanda's happy with their current arrangement. Can Derek convince her a lifetime of nights together will be so much sweeter?

Meet Mr. July ... he's determined to heat things up.

Chapter One

Last year, in July

"HONESTLY, Amanda, I'm fifteen hundred miles away," Jenna Montgomery said, her voice as clear as if she were sitting on the next barstool at The Fix on Sixth. "How am I supposed to assess the situation in Austin all the way from Los Angeles if you don't give me anything to work with?"

Amanda Franklin bit her lower lip, forcing herself not to giggle into her smart phone. *Assess the situation?* The way Jenna was talking, you'd think they were engaging in espionage.

Then again, maybe they were. She'd seen enough movies to know that espionage was a game that centered around a dangerous dance where any misinterpretation of signals could get you killed.

Sounded pretty much like dating to her.

"Is he cute?" Jenna asked.

"Would I be calling if he weren't?"

"Good point. What's he doing now?"

"Tiffany's working his table. He just ordered something. I think—Oh! He wears reading glasses."

"Is that bad?" Jenna asked.

Amanda made a low growling noise. "Nope, and especially not with this guy." He'd been holding the menu when he'd first caught her eye, and she'd assumed he wore glasses as a matter of course. But he'd set the menu aside, then taken off his glasses and tucked them into a case.

At the same time, he'd shifted in his chair. For the second time that night their eyes had met, and she'd been rendered breathless by a pair of pale gray eyes that reflected a heat that belied their stone-cold color.

"That's twice," Amanda said, picking up her Jalapeño Margarita, then putting it right back down when she realized she'd already drained the thing. "This guy. He's…"

"What?" Jenna pressed, as Amanda trailed off, unable to find the right word.

"Intense, I guess. I mean, those eyes are the kind you swipe right for, you know?"

"And you don't think it's your imagination? That he's checking you out, I mean. You said he was sitting with someone. He's not on a date and scoping you out, is he? Because that translates to asshole, and you don't want to go there."

"I don't think so. He's sitting with a gorgeous black guy sipping a whiskey. But I'm not getting a vibe that either of them is gay. On the contrary, I'm getting a dancing lady parts vibe."

"From Mr. Glasses?"

"From both of them, but Glasses is the one who knows I'm alive on the planet. Mr. Whiskey hasn't looked at me once. Glasses has taken a couple of peeks. It's kind of…" She trailed off with a shrug even though Jenna couldn't see her.

"What?"

"Hot," Amanda admitted. She couldn't explain it. But there really was something in the way he looked at her that made her tingle in all the right places. And she had to assume it was because of him. Because goodness knows he wasn't the first guy to shoot her a smoldering glance across the bar.

"You should go for it," Jenna announced. "Or,

actually, never mind. *Damn*. I wish I were there. Doing the BFF thing from long distance sucks."

"It does," Amanda agreed. "But what were you going to say?"

"I don't remember."

Amanda wrinkled her nose. "I smell bullshit." She swiveled the bar stool away from the table so that she was facing the bar, then signaled for Reece to bring her another. One of the bar's managers, he was pouring tonight. "Just tell me," Amanda said into the phone, once again turning her attention to Mr. Glasses.

"I don't know," Jenna said. "Rebound guys can be cathartic and all, but you've been—"

"Whoring around?"

"I didn't say that!" Jenna squealed at the same time that Reece slid a fresh margarita in front of Amanda.

"Who's whoring around?" he asked.

"Jenna," Amanda quipped, surprised by how quickly and intently his expression darkened.

"What the hell?" Jenna sputtered. "Who are you talking to?"

"Your BFF who ranks higher than me. I need to get out of here soon, so I'm going to let you guys gossip while I slam back my drink." She and Jenna said their goodbyes, and she passed the phone to Reece.

Reece grinned as Jenna said something, and Amanda silently motioned for him to bring her the check. Since the two of them could easily talk forever, she figured it was better to go ahead and get it now. Then she took a contemplative sip from her margarita and went back to watching Mr. Glasses.

Rebound guy.

Whoring around.

The words swished around in her head like cartoon ghosts with long, wispy tails.

I didn't say that, Jenna had said. But maybe she should have. Maybe it was true.

With a sigh, Amanda took another sip, enjoying the fiery tang, so much more pleasant on her tongue than the aftertaste of her mistakes.

The truth was, Leo had pretty much destroyed her. And, yes, it had been over nine months since she'd even spoken to the bastard, but that didn't change how much his betrayal had hurt. Her friends only knew that it had been a bad breakup. Even Jenna didn't know that Amanda and Leo had been planning to elope.

But then he'd dropped the bomb, and suddenly she was staring at a man she didn't even know. A man who was saying words like "mistake" and "carried away" and "romantic haze."

Bottom line, everything they had shared had been one big illusion as far as he was concerned. It wasn't really love. He'd never loved her.

Boom. Mic drop. Cue the violins.

And to add insult to injury, she'd lost serious ground in her real estate career because her previous boss had feared that she was going to turn domestic and lose her edge. Instead of offering to sponsor her broker application and pass her his portfolio of clients and leads when he retired, he'd handed it off to an eager single male agent. Not that he'd admitted as much out loud, but Amanda wasn't an idiot.

Then again, maybe she was. She'd fallen for Leo, hadn't she?

Which was why Amanda now looked, but didn't touch.

Okay, not true. She *totally* touched. But she rarely bought the merchandise.

As a real estate agent who focused on high-end properties, networking came with the territory, and so Amanda went out a lot. Dates, business meetings, casual cocktails. Whatever you wanted to call it. With men, those types of meetings often led to a sweet commission, and she was just fine with that. Good for her business and good for her ego.

As for getting naked … well, most of her friends thought she was promiscuous, just because she had a seriously naughty sense of humor. She didn't bother to correct them. What was the point? Even Jenna didn't know the extent of how much Amanda *didn't* fuck around.

The truth was, when Amanda let a guy into her bed, it was only when she was absolutely certain that there was no chance that the night would turn into a thing or that the thing would turn into a relationship.

She was still too anesthetized from cleaning up the wounds from her last relationship. No way was she going under the knife again that quickly.

Besides, why would she sacrifice her best business tool—her status as a single woman—so early in her career? Hell, Leo had done her a favor. She'd been struggling until they'd broken up. Now her bank account was full and shiny.

Yup, her life was finally back on track. All was good. No tweaks needed.

Which meant she needed to stay away from Mr. Glasses. Because she could already tell that there was something compelling about him. Something that would be hard to walk away from. And right now, Amanda simply wasn't at a point in her life where she wanted to stick.

Looking, however, was perfectly acceptable, and as Amanda nursed the last sips of her Jalapeño Margarita, she watched Glasses and Whiskey rise, shake hands, and then head for the door. *Friends,* she decided. Connected by a business relationship that had turned into genuine friendship. They probably didn't golf together, though…

She frowned, considering. *Cycling,* she decided, scoping out their lean, muscled bodies. They got together and went cycling. She'd bet her reputation on it.

Her ability to read people was her secret weapon in the world of real estate, and she hardly ever missed. Leo, of course, had been one very big exception. She'd met him when she sold him a house in West Lake. And she'd missed reading him by a mile.

She swiveled back to the bar, intending to grab her phone and pay her bill, but while her phone was there, the check wasn't.

Once again, she caught Reece's eye and signaled for the check.

"Already taken care of," he said, but he was

midway down the very long bar, and she was sure she must have misunderstood him.

"Sorry, come again?"

He moved closer to her, then nodded across the room, to where Tiffany was pocketing the tip from Mr. Glasses's now-abandoned table.

She almost laughed. At least now she knew that she hadn't been imagining his interest. Still, what a lost opportunity.

It was past six now, and she considered staying and ordering some of Tyree's amazing appetizers and calling them dinner, but she was feeling strangely at loose ends. She wanted to move. To walk. And so she slipped her phone into her purse, waved goodbye to Reece, and headed toward the door.

The moment she turned west on the sidewalk, she saw him. *Mr. Glasses.* He stood just past The Fix, ensuring that anyone inside the bar couldn't see him. And though he held his phone in his hand, as if he'd been checking messages only moments before, now all of his attention was focused on her.

"Another fifteen minutes, and I was going to go back in." He spoke with a Texas drawl so slow and rich, it was almost a caress. It certainly felt like one to Amanda.

With effort, she kept her cool. "Were you waiting for me?"

"I guess that depends on whether you'd find the answer creepy or endearing," he said, and she burst out laughing.

"Let's go with door number three," she said.

"Interesting."

"I can live with that." He took a step toward her, his jeans hugging his thighs as he moved. He wore a white button down, and she could see the outline of a plain T-shirt underneath it. Business casual, Texas-style. He wore his hair closely trimmed, and a dusting of beard stubble highlighted a strong jaw.

The man was a looker, no doubt about that. But it was his eyes that truly caught Amanda's attention. A pale gray that seemed almost silver when they caught the light and were now focused on her with an intensity that was almost a physical caress.

"Why?"

His brows rose. "Why can I live with that?"

She smirked. "Why were you waiting for me?"

The corner of his mouth curved up, and she saw the answer in his eyes. A flare of heat. A spark of desire. There was a world of seduction in that look, and she felt the power of it curl through her, warm and enticing.

"Can I buy you a drink?"

She wasn't sure what she expected him to say, but considering the way the air was currently crackling between them, it wasn't that.

Amused, she looked back over her shoulder to the windows of The Fix. "I think you just did."

"Good point. You're welcome."

Laughing, she nodded. "And yes. Thank you."

"You're welcome, and I can offer other options. Whiskey, for example. Or Amy's Ice Cream."

"Tempting," she admitted, laughing at the juxtaposition.

His eyes caught and captured hers. "Or we could simply talk. Just name your pleasure. What do you say?"

She drew in a breath, aroused by the innocent words and the not so innocent tone in which he'd delivered them. She slid her hands along her skirt, drying her palms . "Why?"

His lips twitched. "If you don't know, the answer is probably no. Too bad for me."

She considered lying. After all, this guy was too appealing—she could tell that right away. It would be too easy to enjoy his company. To get twisted up in something inconvenient and complicated that she neither wanted nor needed right now.

But then he smiled, and she found herself smiling back. "Yeah," she said. "A drink sounds great."

He nodded toward the door. "After you?"

As much as she loved the drinks at The Fix, she was tight with too many people there. By the time she and Mr. Glasses parted ways, Reece would have undoubtedly called Jenna, and Amanda would have half a dozen texts or voicemails.

"Got another suggestion?"

"I do," he said. "How about the Winston Hotel?"

"Perfect." The Austin location of the Texas-based international chain of high-end hotels was only a short walk from The Fix and boasted an elegant bar. "I'm Amanda, by the way." She extended her hand.

He took it, and a coil of pure lust curled through her. *Yeah. There was definitely chemistry.* "Derek," he said, and from the tone of his voice she couldn't tell if he'd been equally affected by their connection. But he held her hand a little longer than etiquette required, and when he finally pulled away, Amanda had to fight a tangible wave of disappointment.

"Are you local?" she asked as they walked down Brazos toward the river

He shook his head. "No, but I love Austin. I come here a lot for business. That's why I'm here now, actually." He paused long enough to catch her eye. "I leave for Dallas tomorrow morning."

"Oh." Most women wouldn't perk up when they learned their date for the evening was geographically undesirable. But Amanda was not most women. And as far as she was concerned, Mr. Derek Glasses's appeal had just spiked up a notch or two.

She smiled at him. "Then I guess it's lucky we met."

"Yeah," he said, looking at her with the kind of undeniable heat designed to make a woman melt. "Very lucky, indeed."

Chapter Two

"SO ARE you some sort of movie star?"

Amanda asked the question as a joke, but she would've believed him if the answer was yes. They'd been seated at a secluded table in the small bar for only fifteen minutes and from the reaction of the staff and a few of the customers, he seemed to be the main attraction. Couple that with those sultry, heavy-lidded gray eyes and the sensual way his body moved, and Amanda figured her guess couldn't be too far off.

The corner of his mouth quirked up with amusement. "I'm flattered," he said. "But what on earth makes you say that?"

"Well, you're gorgeous, for one thing."

"I'm glad you think so. I've been thinking the same thing about you all night. How stunning you look in that perfectly tailored skirt. And how exceptional I'm sure you'd look out of it."

It was Amanda's turn to be amused. "Not bad," she said, then slipped her foot out of her shoe and rubbed her toes along his ankle. "But if you think a lame compliment like that is going to get me into bed, you're going to have to try harder."

He'd just lifted his whiskey glass to his lips. Fortunately, he hadn't taken a sip, because a low, throaty laugh bubbled out, the sound deliciously sexy. "Noted," he said. "I'll work on my pick-up lines."

"You do that." She took a sip of her own wine to hide her smile. She wasn't entirely sure what was going on between her and this guy, but she did know that she enjoyed his company and his sense of humor. Somehow—she honestly wasn't sure what the trigger had been—they'd slid from polite date talk into teasing sexual innuendoes during their walk to the hotel.

Under any other circumstances, she would have put the brakes on that right away, even with the sexual chemistry that crackled between them. She had her rules, after all. But this guy, with his out of town address and departure date of tomorrow, seemed like a safe bet. A good risk.

More important, she wanted him.

And it had been a long time since she truly, really, fully craved a man.

"Also," she said, her toes on his ankle again, "I think you need to lose a few points for that lame attempt at avoiding my original question."

"I'm not a movie star," he said. "That wasn't a serious question, was it?"

She lifted a shoulder. "Ever since we walked into this hotel, the staff's had their eye on you. And the service is excellent. You must be somebody."

"Oh, I am."

"Who?"

He leaned forward, his expression so intense it made her heart skip a beat. "I'm the man who's going to make you beg."

Her mouth went suddenly dry. "Oh."

She swallowed, her entire body flush with desire. She wanted to melt right then. To tell him to take her to a room and prove all his big talk.

But Amanda also didn't like to lose, and what had started out as teasing now felt like a game. A decadent, seductive, fabulous game. And she knew exactly what her next move was.

Slowly, she eased her foot up his leg, her eyes never leaving his until her toes were resting between his legs, his cock getting stiffer by the second. Their small table had a cloth, so her ministrations were hidden under white, draping fabric. But anyone looking at his face could make a good guess as to what was happening under that curtain.

"Poor thing," she said, faking a frown. "All trapped inside there. Maybe you should unzip and let him come out and play."

She watched him catch his breath, then sit up straighter, obviously working for control. "You're cheating," he accused.

Amanda lifted her brows. "How?"

"If I could think right now, I'd tell you."

She laughed, completely surprised. "I like you." She spoke without thinking, but what the hell, it was true. Then she picked up her glass and tossed back her wine. "And oh, look. I'm all finished with my drink."

He did the same, setting the empty highball glass back on the table with a bang. "What do you know? I'm done, too."

With a wicked smile, she pulled her foot away. "I guess the question now is, which one of us is going to beg. And for what?"

"I have no shame," he countered, taking her

hand and gently stroking her thumb. "Come to my room with me. I'm begging you."

"You talked me into it," she said, melting from the sensation of his thumb brushing her skin.

"Come on." He slid out of the chair, and she dipped her eyes to his package, then flashed him a completely unapologetic grin.

"We should get you to a room."

"That's my plan." He shifted a bit, as if uncomfortable, then started to walk toward the elevator. She walked beside him, fighting a smile.

"You do realize the trouble you've gotten yourself in? Punishment might be swift and harsh."

"A girl can dream."

He chuckled.

"Don't you need to sign the check?"

He shook his head. "They know me."

"If you say so..."

He laughed. "I promise. It's all good. And right now, I really don't want to wait."

That was a sentiment she could get fully behind, and she fell in beside him as they walked to the elevator. He took her hand as they stepped on, along with another couple so laden down with shopping bags they had to be tourists.

He stood with his back to the wall and tugged

her in front of him, then wrapped his arms around her waist as he pulled her close, nestling them together so tightly that she could feel his erection against the small of her back.

The other couple stood close to the doors, as if wanting to ensure a quick escape. Which meant they weren't looking behind them. Which was probably why they didn't notice when one of Derek's hands snaked over her pelvis, coming to rest right on her pubic bone.

Between that pressure and the sensation of his cock against her back, Amanda half-feared she might explode right then and there. Her body tingled all over, and she was hyperaware of every point of contact with Derek.

She longed to strip naked and feel skin on skin, but that wasn't happening. Not quite yet, anyway. Instead, she bit her lower lip, swallowed, and tried to decide if she hoped the ride to their floor would be fast or very, very slow.

As it turned out, the ride was fast. They were on seven, but so was the other couple. Which meant that there was no privacy for anything more than the intimate position they'd shared in the elevator.

That was enough. As foreplay went, it was pretty damn effective, because by the time they stepped out of the car, Amanda's breasts were tight and sensitive, and her sex ached with a potent need.

As far as she was concerned, he couldn't get the door open fast enough. And when he finally did push it open, she barely had time to hope that things would move fast before he'd pulled her roughly to him and was pulling at her shirt, tugging the light silk shell over her head.

He looked at her then, just for a moment. A sigh slipped from his mouth, and he breathed, "You're so damn beautiful."

"Please," she begged, her own fingers working to untuck his shirt. To feel the hard muscles of his abs beneath her skin.

"I want to touch you. You—oh, God, Amanda, there's something about you that burns inside me. I can't wait. Or maybe I can, but I damn sure don't want to."

"Me neither," she admitted. "Where's your bedroom?"

He took her hand and led them both there. Then he tilted his head as if inspecting her.

"What?"

"I seem to recall you needing a punishment."

"Oh, really? What did you have in mind?"

"Strip for me."

She shook her head. "Nope." She walked in front of him, then stood just inches from where he sat. She wore her heels, her skirt and her bra. Underwear, too, if a tiny, soaked thong counted.

Slowly, she sucked in the tip of her finger. Then she slid it down under the waistband of her skirt to her clit, teasing herself for him to watch. He couldn't see what she was doing, of course, but it didn't matter. His eyes were on her, and the desire she saw there—wild, feral—made her so much wetter.

"You want? Then you undress me." She turned, giving him access to the zipper.

"Baby, I think we're going to have a very good time." He tugged the zipper down, then eased the skirt over her hips. "Beautiful," he murmured, stroking her ass. "Spread your legs, then bend over for me and grab your ankles."

She did, and he got to his knees, then ran his tongue over the curve of her ass as he tugged her thong down, fully exposing her.

So aroused she couldn't stand it, she bit her lower lip, afraid she'd come the moment he touched her. She didn't—but when he ran his tongue up her perineum, she almost lost her mind and begged him to fuck her.

"I told you I'd make you beg," he said, making her laugh even though she wanted to beg him some more.

He moved away to the nightstand and returned with a condom. "I don't know how long I can wait," he said, as he sheathed himself. Then he unfastened her bra and she wriggled out of it, moaning in pleasure as his hot hands cupped her breasts.

He played with her nipples as he moved his hips, stroking her from behind with the length of his erection.

"You are so hot, Amanda," he said, and her name on his lips made her want him even more.

"I want to see you." She turned around, standing naked now except for her heels. She put her hand flat on his chest, and pushed him to a seated position on the edge of the bed. Then she crawled on top of him so that her sex rubbed his erection as she closed her mouth over his, longing for another slow, consuming kiss.

"No more, he said, roughly breaking the kiss. "I've got to be inside you."

She laughed, then kissed him quick. "Now we're tied. You begged, too."

"Vixen." He held her by the hips as he positioned her, teasing her core with his tip until he was one more point ahead because she'd begged for him to release her so that she could lower herself and take him all in.

Since he wanted it just as badly, he didn't argue, and soon he was filling her as she rode him, her ankles crossed behind his back, and her hands at his hips so that she could pull him in deeper, too.

"That's it, baby," he said, then closed his mouth on hers, sucking and teasing, then slipping one hand off her hip to move between them and rub her clit as their bodies pistoned together.

Wild electric shivers began to break through her, long threads of electricity that were coalescing in her core. She arched back, and he took her breast in his mouth, then sucked, so hard and with such intensity that she felt the reverberations all the way in her sex.

Mostly, she felt on fire. Her body alive. Aware. "I'm close," she told him. "Come with me. Derek, please come with me."

He said nothing, but she watched his face as the storm approached. A violent passion that was playing out over his features, so alight with pleasure. A pleasure that she'd brought to him. That they'd created together.

It felt magical—and as the thought entered her mind, that's when she exploded, rocking harder against him, wanting that extra friction to take her even further before they both ended up gasping and sated, their bodies limp on the still fully-made bed.

"Wow," Amanda said when she could breathe again. She shifted until she was facing him, their legs twined together. "I mean, seriously, *wow.*"

Derek grinned. "I'll take that as a compliment."

"You should." She eased toward him and kissed him. "I had a lovely time tonight."

"That sounds like a goodbye."

"Early meeting tomorrow." It was true, or else Amanda might have been tempted to stay. She realized then that she'd never told him what she did. Despite the fact that he clearly had money and might have a lead on more clients. Or be a client himself.

That *really* wasn't like her, and the realization was a little unnerving.

"You okay? Looks like I lost you there."

"What? Oh." She kissed him again lightly to cover her distraction, then slipped out of bed. "My mind shifted into work mode. To be honest, I shouldn't have taken the time tonight—I have a lot of preparing to do." She flashed a genuine smile. "But I don't regret it at all."

"Glad to hear it. Neither do I."

He stayed on the bed, his eyes on her as she wriggled into her panties. Honestly, it was like doing a reverse strip tease, and for a moment she was tempted to change in the bathroom. But the approval and desire on his face erased all thoughts of escaping out of sight. On the contrary, she was tempted to yank the skirt up, crawl back into bed, and straddle him.

Down girl.

"I never did answer your question."

"I know you're not in Hollywood," she said as she shrugged into her blouse. "But now I'm going with rock star. Your performance tonight was incredible."

"I'm glad you liked the concert." He tossed the sheet aside, then walked naked to her, his hard body distracting her so thoroughly her fingers fumbled on the button of her skirt.

His cocky grin suggested that he knew exactly why she was having a hard time, and he took over the job, his fingers brushing her heated skin as he slowly zipped and buttoned the skirt. "All dressed now. Seems a shame to cover up such a lovely view."

"Well, maybe you can take another peek sometime."

The moment the words were out of her mouth, Amanda froze. She hadn't intended to say that—the whole point of tonight was that it was a one-off. A way to scratch an itch without getting mired in complications.

Point being, she'd expected and intended this to be a one-off. But then he said that he got to Austin every few months for work and asked if he could call her. And the only answer that sprang to her lips was, "Yes."

"Good," he said, that simple word conveying so much emotion it seemed to wash over her.

"I should tell you, though. I don't do relation-ships. My business is my relationship right now, you know? It's where my focus is. Something like today would be fun."

"Indeed it would," he said,

"Here." She pulled a card from her purse and handed it to him. "Business and cell." She licked her lips, then bit the bullet. "I really do hope you call."

"I will," he said.

She smiled, feeling awkward and a little giddy, then headed for the door. She'd just turned the lock, when he spoke again.

"I never did answer you."

"I know a lost cause when I see one," she quipped, then added, "Actually, don't tell me now. If we don't see each other again, it doesn't matter. And if we do, you can tell me then."

Still naked, he crossed to her in four long strides, his eyes never leaving her face. Without a word, he pulled her to him, then made her legs go weak under the force of his hot, demanding kiss.

When he released her, she was breathing hard, her body begging her to chuck work for the day and spend it in bed.

His smile suggested he knew exactly what she was thinking, but all he said was, "It's a deal."

Chapter Three

ANTHONY WINSTON TOOK a sip of orange juice as he studied his son.

The ritual was familiar, if unpleasant, and Derek sat up straight and stayed quiet, letting his father see whatever he'd see. Not that the inspection mattered much. In Derek's experience, his father saw what he wanted to, not what was there.

With Derek, Anthony saw a screw-up. A man more interested in having a good time than working for the family business. Which had been true a decade ago.

But he was thirty-six now, and things had changed. The family business was important to him, something that he proved every day in the office, where he did one hell of a fine job, if he did say so himself.

He *had* to say so himself, because his father damn sure never did.

And then there was Derek's sister, Melinda. Derek loved her dearly, but Mellie was a flake. In Anthony's eyes, however, she could do no wrong. According to the elder Winston, the fiasco with the pool remodel she was supposedly overseeing at the Winston family ranch had nothing to do with her scatterbrained tendencies. As far as Anthony was concerned, the construction manager had been entirely at fault. Not his precious Mellie.

Of course, Anthony Winston's vision was much more clear where his business was concerned. There, every detail was seen, analyzed, and comprehended in meticulous detail.

Which begged the question of why, if Derek was such a screw-up, was he the one going to Austin to negotiate with the owners of the South Congress Motor Inn. True, the deal had been Derek's idea, but Anthony Winston liked to be in the thick of things. He wasn't the type to hand off negotiations simply because someone else had conceived a project.

Could it be that underneath the constant criticism, his father had a clearer vision than Derek had realized?

He didn't know. All he knew was that if he screwed it up, his father would have his head on a platter, breaded and fried for lunch. Probably served with a nice Chianti.

Now, Anthony took another sip of juice, then scowled when Derek finished off his cup of coffee. "You should drink your juice, not coffee. That's your third cup. Too much caffeine dulls the senses. You need to be sharp."

Derek bit back a sigh, ignoring his still-full juice glass. "I'm sharp, Dad. Sharp enough to know that you didn't order me to the ranch this morning just so you could criticize my caffeine habit."

The ranch was Winston Ranch, four hundred and ten acres in the Oak Cliff neighborhood of the City of Dallas. Right then, Derek and his father were under the cabana by the pool being served breakfast by a waitstaff so efficient every one of them could have worked at any top New York restaurant. They didn't, though, because Anthony Winston paid them too well.

Years ago, the ranch had spread out over a much larger area and had been an actual working ranch. But that was before Derek's time, and he only knew about it because the sale of that excess land, coupled with his great-grandfather's decision to build a showpiece hotel in downtown Dallas, had been the catalyst for the Winston family fortune. Which, frankly, was vast.

Now, the ranch served as the family home, with the main house, his sister's smaller home, a twenty-car garage, and a few scattered cottages for the staff. Fifteen acres stood in Derek's name, waiting for him to build a home, too. But that wasn't something he intended to do. He enjoyed working in the family business, but he wanted his own niche. And that meant focusing on new directions at the Winston corporation, many of which took him away from Dallas. More important, he had no desire to live on the ranch, where every time he looked to the sky, all he'd see was his father's eye looking down into the microscope. He got enough of that from working with the man.

Anthony put down his juice glass and silently sat back in his chair, studying Derek. His father was a big man, with the same broad shoulders that Derek saw every time he looked in a mirror. He could also be intimidating as hell.

Today, Derek wasn't intimidated. Quite the opposite. Today, he was irritated. "I need to get to the airport. Why the summons to the castle?"

"Because the reputation of this company

requires that the South Congress Motor Inn deal be handled with finesse."

Derek leaned back, his fingers steepled. "Have you forgotten that I originated this deal? That the entire concept driving this acquisition was mine?"

His father sighed. "You've got a good mind, son, no one doubts that."

Derek's brows lifted; as far as he'd known, his father doubted it on a daily basis.

"But this is a deal that needs to be handled quietly. We don't need chatter among the investors or speculation in the trades." Anthony met Derek's eyes. "You understand what I'm saying?"

"Dad, I've been in this business since I was in diapers. I have business degrees from Harvard and Yale. You sent me off to work at competing hotels when I was sixteen years old. I've delivered room service. I've worked in the laundry. And I make one hell of a fine concierge if I do say so myself. I know this business top to bottom. Plus, I'm the one who conceived Winston Boutiques. So forgive me if I sound a little put-out for being lectured about what I already know."

The Winston Boutiques division was still in the planning stages, but Derek had every intention of bringing it to fruition and making it his own. And right now, everything hinged on the South Congress Motor Inn deal. The idea was to find well-located but financially burdened motels with sentimental significance to their town, refurbish them into quality rooms with high-end amenities, and market them as premier destination accommodations with a retro feel.

Last month, he'd scoped out the failing motor inn on Austin's extremely retail-and-tourist friendly South Congress Avenue, and he'd decided it was the perfect launch location.

All Derek had to do was acquire the place and get the ball rolling.

And when he nailed this project, he intended to insist that he be put in charge of the entire Winston Boutiques division.

That, however, was ultimately up to the board of directors. And the board didn't wipe their own asses without first hearing what Anthony Winston wanted.

He sighed. Basically, he was stuck at the ranch until his father said his piece.

"I'm not doubting your skill, son. You're a Winston, and you've got the chops. But we don't want the press to get wind of what we're doing, and the way you and Jared Ingram behave…"

Derek held up a hand. "What the hell does Jared have to do with anything? He's in LA, and I'm here, and I haven't gone out with him in months."

"Good to know," his father said. "Because you boys need to calm down."

Jared Ingram had been Derek's boarding school roommate. The heir to a family fortune that reached back to the beginning of time, Jared had enough money to buy and sell Anthony Winston a thousand times over. He was smart and funny and personable—and unlike Derek, he didn't have a clue what he wanted to do with his life.

"Calm down?" Derek stared at his father. "Is that a euphemism for being seen? For having a good time? Christ, Dad, I've spent my entire life running interference for the Winston brand. You're going to begrudge me a few parties?"

"It's a euphemism for screwing around and making an ass of yourself. What? You don't know how to have a good time without partying with some floozy? Getting drunk and getting your face in the papers every time you're with that boy?"

Frustrated, Derek leaned back and ran his fingers through his hair.

No doubt, Jared was a player. And although

Derek could never steal Jared's crown in that regard, he couldn't deny that he used to walk in those shoes, too. Especially when he was in the city with Jared.

Jared was not, however, a bad guy or a wastrel, and his father's suggestion to the contrary made Derek's blood boil. "I work hard. I play hard. And I have never once shirked my responsibilities to the Winston Corporation."

Even as he said them, though, the words seemed hollow. The truth was, Jared's antics had been getting on his nerves lately, too. For the last year, Derek had been going out with his friend more to keep an eye on him. Not to join him.

But it was just like his dad not to give him the benefit of the doubt.

Still, he had to admit that his father had a point. Just because Derek wasn't getting wasted at every club from New York to Dallas to Los Angeles didn't mean that Derek was entirely pure. He'd had his share of women over the years, and continued to do so. And, yeah, sometimes a piece of that ended up in the papers.

His past shouldn't impact the Austin deal … but if the past became the present, it might. If he was seen with a woman in Austin, that would undoubtedly end up on social media. Not harmful in and of itself, but an observant competitor might see a picture of him in Austin and wonder what he was doing there. Possibly investigate. Possibly figure it out.

And then the Winston Corporation could find itself in a multiple party bidding war instead of being the only player at the table opposite the motor inn.

Damn, but the world had been simpler in his father's time. But there was no putting the cork in the social media bottle.

Begrudgingly, he downed his glass of orange juice, then stood up, meeting his father's eyes. "I'm heading to the airport now," he said. "And I'm not going to fuck this up."

And he wouldn't, he thought as he headed around the pool and toward the main house. But the frustrating reality was that he'd intended to call Amanda Franklin from the road to let her know he'd be in town for the night.

For over a month now, she'd filled his head. And memories of their night together had invaded his dreams, so intense that on more than one occasion he'd had to take a cold shower before he even thought about getting dressed.

He'd resisted calling her from Dallas over the last month. She'd made it perfectly clear that if they got together again it would only be a drive-by. But he was okay with that. As much as she filled his thoughts, he didn't need the complication of a steady woman in his life.

On the contrary, for years, he'd been the guy who'd gone out with a different woman every weekend. Not with quite the exuberance of Jared, maybe, but Derek had never been the type to stick. What was the point? His business was his priority, and it ate up his time. Why not enjoy the rare free time that he had? Especially when there were so many women in all of Winston's various flagship cities who were more than happy to keep him entertained.

And the fact that he hadn't called a single one of them in the last month had nothing to do with the night he and Amanda had spent together. Why would it? She was cut from the same cloth, wasn't she? A woman focusing on her career and not looking for a relationship.

So no. The only reason for his relative celibacy these last four weeks had been the insanity of his schedule. He'd been pulling long hours planning the new division and working on the terms of the motor inn deal. And at no time during those weeks had he crossed paths with any women interesting enough to pull him away from work.

Amanda was interesting enough.

The words sang through him. *True enough.*

And that, of course, was why she was still on his radar.

As he drew closer to the house, he texted the butler to request that a driver and car be waiting for him by the time he'd grabbed his overnight bag from the trunk of his Mercedes. He'd leave his car here so that he could catch up on emails during the drive from the ranch to the Winston hanger at Love Field.

They'd been on the road for fifteen minutes, and Derek had managed to answer all of the morning's emails, when his phone rang. He glanced at the Caller ID, intending to ignore it unless it was his assistant, only to see that it was Jared.

"Where are you this week?"

"Aspen. You should come. The snow's cold, but the women are hot."

Derek chuckled. "I guess so. I thought you were in LA. Weren't you all excited about optioning some author's book to turn into a movie?"

"She was hot, too. But it didn't work out."

There was an unfamiliar edge in Jared's tone. "What's going on, man?"

"Nothing. Shit. Seriously, it's no big thing."

"What isn't?"

"Carla. The author. Like I said, no big thing."

From Jared's tone, it sounded like it was a big thing.

"What happened?"

"She dumped me."

Derek's eyes widened. "I didn't know you were dating her?"

"I wasn't. Maybe that was the problem. She dumped me as a producer. Said she didn't trust me with the project. That I was fly-by-night."

From Derek's point of view, Carla sounded like a sharp woman. Jared had never worked in Hollywood, but he had the money to play. He'd gotten the itch to be a producer, which could turn out fine if he paid quality people to work with him. But from what Derek had seen, Jared was acting, not working. Playing the producer role without actually accomplishing anything except getting his face known at all the hottest clubs and a few mentions in *The Hollywood Reporter*.

"So I said fuck it and came to Colorado. You

should come. I've met some lovely ladies who are happy to help me stay warm."

"No can do. About to catch a plane to Austin."
And he wouldn't go even if he could.

"Too bad. This is the life, my friend. Working in Hollywood was way too much trouble. Not worth the time if you don't need the scratch." But for the first time, there was something in Jared's voice that made him think that his friend didn't believe his own bullshit.

"You okay?"

"Just tired. Keeping busy, you know?"

The zing was back in Jared's voice, and the shadow of worry that had settled over Derek started to dissipate.

"Fair enough. We're at the airport, so I'll talk to you later."

"Get your ass up to the city. It's been too long."

It had, but Derek hadn't been in the mood for Manhattan lately. Instead, it had been Austin on his mind.

All he said, though, was, "Sure."

Chapter Four

AS FAR AS Amanda was concerned, the only real downside of her job was that she couldn't justify not answering her phone. She'd long ago decided against carrying two mobile phones, and that meant that she gave her number out freely to clients, potential clients, and other agents and brokers. Which meant that she ended up answering so many texts that she'd trained herself to dictate responses. It was either that or start wearing her nails short. And that really wasn't happening.

The phone calls were the worst, though. She was always happy to talk about real estate, even if the buyer was unqualified or just looking. After all, you never knew when their circumstances would change, and she wanted to be at the top of their call list. But that meant she had to answer all unfamiliar numbers, too, since it might be a potential client who'd been given her card.

As a result, she'd been on the receiving end of more scam calls and robocalls than any sane person should be subjected to. Calls about things she didn't care about. Calls about things she didn't want.

And sometimes, she even got unexpected calls about things she shouldn't care about, and things she shouldn't want. Like the call this morning. The one she'd answered, only to be serenaded by Derek's slow drawl. "Good morning, gorgeous. Do you know who this is?"

Did she?

No doubt about that. And apparently every part of her had known it, too. Because as he'd continued to tell her about how he was boarding a plane for Austin and he'd be free from his meetings and dinners by ten and could meet her at ten-fifteen, her body had begun to ache with unfamiliar, but not unwelcome, longing.

With a sigh, she stood in the ornate lobby of the Winston Hotel and looked down at the screen of her phone, checking the time for the thousandth time. *One minute past when she'd last looked.*

Amanda sighed, then waited.

It had been a month since she and Derek had

met outside The Fix and shared that incredible night, and though she'd told herself over and over that it would be best if he never called again—best to not get involved—she couldn't deny the rush of heat that had coursed through her when she'd heard his voice. A heat that had morphed into anticipation when he'd asked her to meet him at the Winston at a quarter past ten.

"Room 715," he'd said, naming a room on the same floor they'd gone to last time, and she'd promised to be there exactly on the dot.

Now it was seven after ten, and she kept checking the clock on her phone like an idiot. "Eager, much?" she chided herself softly. Because, of course, she was.

That was the reason she'd almost told him that she had plans tonight. Because despite essentially suggesting that they should see each other again, she really hadn't expected to hear from him. Had, in fact, thought it would be best if they both just backed away slowly.

Yet she hadn't said no. On the contrary, she'd very eagerly said yes. And all because there'd been such intense sparks between them. And not just sexually. They'd laughed and talked. They'd clicked.

And the sex had been off the charts.

Which, of course, was why she was here. And why she kept telling herself she should go away.

Derek was the kind of guy who could get under her skin, and she had no time for a relationship.

Not that they'd talked about any of that last time, but she was going to have to say something tonight. They needed to be clear. If this was going to be something they repeated, then it needed to be about the sex. Nothing else.

She just hoped that they reached an agreement … not to mention a mind-blowing orgasm.

SHE KNOCKED AT EXACTLY TEN-FIFTEEN, and he opened the door ten seconds later. The moment he did, Amanda knew there'd be no trouble granting the orgasm part of her wish. The man looked as hot as sin in black jeans, bare feet, and a pale gray T-shirt that clung to his chest and showed off his well-developed arms.

Not a bad view to be faced with, but it was the expression on his face that made Amanda certain she was going to suffer no regrets for keeping this date. An almost feral intensity that had her pulse pounding and small beads of sweat popping up on the back of her neck.

"Hi," she said. Or, rather, she tried to. She didn't actually get the word out before he'd tugged her into the entry hall, kicked the door shut, then pinned her against the wall.

Immediately, his mouth crushed against hers, all teeth and lips and tongue. It was a demand, a promise. Lust and longing. Hell, it was sex. The most oral kind of sex that Amanda could imagine, and all she wanted to do was get lost in it.

His fingers twined in her hair, holding her steady as his tongue did battle with her own. Their teeth clashed and she tasted blood, tangy and undeniably arousing in the moment.

He'd held her trapped against the wall as his mouth ravaged hers, and the simple knowledge that he'd taken control—that he was taking *her*—made her even more aroused, though she was astounded that was even possible. Her panties were soaked, and her entire body was aroused, on edge. As if one touch could send her spinning out into space. And oh, how she wanted to spin.

Unexpectedly, he pulled away, just long enough to capture her eyes in his gaze. Then he moved his hands, sliding down along her arms, bare in the silk tank top she'd worn.

His touch made her shiver, and she drew in a breath, her lips parted as she closed her eyes, wanting simply to feel. His hands on her arms. His body, lean and muscled, pressed tight against hers. His erection, straining against his jeans and pressing insistently into her lower belly.

Thank God she'd worn a skirt, because she couldn't stand this much longer. "Please," she begged. "I want you now. Hard and deep and right here against this wall."

He pulled back long enough so she could see the gleam of pure arousal in his eyes. Then he reached down and grabbed her skirt and in one violent motion thrust it up around her waist.

He lifted her next, so that her legs encircled him and her back was pressed to the wall. He was strong, thank goodness, and he used one hand to free himself, then dug a condom out of his back pocket.

"I came prepared," he said.

"Show me your mad skills and get it on fast."

He did just that, and she would have applauded, except she was too busy screaming his name when he drove forward, burying himself inside her in one long thrust that claimed her and tamed her and filled every cell inside her.

He pounded into her, her back slamming against the wall, their mouths banging together. It was wild and dirty and exactly what she wanted. And when the explosion finally came, she cried out his name and clung to him like he was her everything. In that moment, maybe he was.

Slowly, he lowered them both to the floor, and though she knew they ought to move, all she could manage was to lay there and breath.

Oh, yeah. That was good.

"Hey," he murmured, propping himself up on one elbow. "Nice to see you."

She burst out laughing, but the sound seemed strangled since he'd reduced her to a limp, boneless creature. Laughter really wasn't in the cards. "You, too," she managed.

With effort, she rose up on her elbows, then looked around. "Is this the same room?"

He flashed a devious grin as he stood up. "We had such good luck with it the first time."

"Just think how amazing it'll be in the same room *and* the same bed," she quipped.

"I'm ready if you are."

Her eyes went wide, and she looked down,

noticing that he hadn't been kidding about being ready. She bit her lower lip, and he shrugged.

"Saves getting dressed for conversation only to get undressed again later."

She had to fight not to laugh. "I really don't understand your earth logic, but I like the plan. Lead the way."

———

DEREK TOOK a sip of wine from the abandoned glass he'd left on the bedside table. Between the two of them, they'd killed off a bottle in record time. Then again, they'd been thirsty after their workout. Their second workout, if you counted the hall. Which he absolutely did.

He allowed himself a self-satisfied grin, then stretched out in the bed next to Amanda, who was dozing beside him. Gently, he brushed his fingertips over her pale skin as he reveled in the way she squirmed under his touch.

"Stop," she murmured. "You're tickling me."

"Maybe that's my plan. Maybe I want to wake you up."

She rolled over, blinking at him. "So that I'll get out of your hair?"

Her words were like a kick in his gut. "You can stay as long as you want. I was thinking wakefulness might lead to other activities."

"You're insatiable."

"And you have a dirty mind," he countered. "I was talking about conversation." He cocked his head toward the suite's living room. "Want to go sip some wine? Talk? Watch a movie?"

For a moment, she looked tempted. Then she shook her head. "I should probably—" She cut herself off as she sat up in bed, pulling the sheet tight over her breasts. "It's just that I have a showing at nine tomorrow, and there's a ton of prep before hand, and—"

He pressed his fingertip to her lips. "It's okay. No explanation required."

She seemed to melt a little, and he thought he saw a plea in her eyes.

"Really."

She studied him for a moment, then nodded before slipping out of bed. He watched her dress, regretting ever saying a word, because then she might have fallen asleep, and he could have awakened with her in his arms.

Then again, if they'd done that, she'd probably be late for her showing tomorrow. Assuming she actually had a showing tomorrow. It was just as likely that he'd spooked her and she was running.

That was okay, though. She could run. For now.

He just wanted her to run back the next time he was in town.

When she was dressed, he got up and pulled on his briefs, then grabbed the Winston Hotel logo robe and tugged it on as they walked toward the door.

She paused with her hand on the knob. "I really am sorry."

"Don't even think about it." He leaned against the wall. "Actually, I'll be in town again in about a month. For that matter, lately I've been coming to Austin on a pretty regular basis." Not an outright lie, and his trips really were about to become more frequent.

"We could play it by ear." He swallowed, then forged ahead. "Or we could plan on it. This room. I can text you the dates as soon as I know them."

Good God, had he really just suggested that? He needed more sleep. Or possibly less alcohol.

Her eyes widened, and he thought he might get lost in the flicker of gold in those deep brown pools.

"This room? How can you be sure you'll always get this room?"

"Ah, right. Remember how you cut me off before I could say what I did for a living?"

She nodded.

"Well, my job more or less involves being a Winston."

"Come again?"

He managed a straight face. "Only if you stay a little longer."

She rolled her eyes. "Behave. And what are you talking about?"

"Derek Winston," he said, extending his hand to hers. "And my family owns this hotel."

"Oh. *Oh.*" She tugged her hand free, then twirled a lock of hair around her finger, seeming to process that info. "And so you want to use this room for a standing hook-up?"

He held up a hand. "Hold on, I didn't mean it that way."

"No, no. I get it." She nodded slowly, her brow furrowed in thought.

Then she surprised him by stepping forward and kissing his cheek. "You know what? I think that arrangement will work just fine."

Chapter Five

BY SEPTEMBER, the Winston Boutiques project had stalled, which was frustrating, and both his father and the board seemed to be losing interest in it.

"I'm not giving up on it," he told his father on a Friday afternoon as he stood soldier-straight in front of the older man's office.

"Then don't. But you're going to have to pursue it on your own time."

Derek nodded, considering. He could do that. Fly down on weekends. Arrange more meetings. Show to the reluctant buyers that he was going to improve the property, not destroy it.

And then, if there was any spare time, he could see Amanda.

The thought made him pause. In July, he'd been

having drinks at The Fix with his friend Landon, and Amanda had caught his eye. Since then, Amanda had gone from a silent extra in the movie of his life to having the female lead.

Since he'd met her, he never thought about pursuing another woman, and as he pondered that new attitude, he decided he was okay with it. As far as women went, he'd yet to meet one who aroused, amused, and challenged him as much as she did.

Maybe that was odd, considering he still knew so little about her outside of bed, but as far as Derek was concerned, all that meant was that there was a lot more juice to come.

He nodded. "Fair enough. My own time, then. Tomorrow's Saturday. I'll head down then." He started to turn away, but his father called him back.

"There's one more thing we need to talk about."

Derek paused by the door, his brows raised in question.

"As you know, Lawrence is moving to the European division. That leaves the position of Director of North American Operations open. I'd like you to take it."

"I see."

Inside, Derek's heart was pounding. The position was one of huge responsibility, but it was also a lot of work. And while his struggling Winston Boutiques project would fall under the umbrella of the new job, he'd have limited time to work on it.

On top of that, the job required extensive travel as it required in-person visits to all the Winston properties on a regular, rotating basis. That was one of the corporate policies his great-grandfather had instituted when the company had expanded past that first hotel, and as far as every Winston who'd run the company was concerned, it was sacrosanct.

A burdensome job. But an important one.

And it would take him to Austin at least once each month. Maybe more.

He blinked, then shook his head to erase the thought.

Neither Amanda Franklin nor his libido should play any part in this decision.

Even so…

"I'll take it," he said, and was rewarded by a flare of pride in his father's eyes.

"THANKS FOR DINNER, MOM," Amanda said, as she started to clear the dishes. "Awesome as usual."

As far as Amanda was concerned, her mother made the world's best lasagna.

"You can wait on that, sweetie," her mom said, nodding at the dishes. "Come join us in the living room?"

"No, it's okay. I'll do this, then I may take a quick walk down to the water."

She tried to keep her voice normal, but the truth was that she was on edge. She'd arrived a few hours earlier for a Friday dinner with her parents and Nolan, her stepbrother. While her mother cooked, she'd been in the living room checking her emails while her dad and brother watched ESPN.

That's when she'd gotten Derek's text that he'd be in Austin on Saturday, and did she want to join him for breakfast in their room?

She'd quickly tapped out a yes, then hesitated before sending it. No need to look too eager, after all. Especially when they weren't really dating.

It was the *not dating* thing that was twisting her up now, and she was glad of the mindless task of clearing the table. She would have liked to have loaded the machine herself, too, but Nolan came in and offered to help, and that was such a rare thing that she agreed.

They finished the work silently, although she

had the strange impression that he had something to ask her, and when they were done, he went back into the living room to join their parents.

She went the other direction, pouring herself a glass of wine, then walking outside to sit on the dock, dangle her feet into the water, and wonder what it was that she and Derek were doing.

"So what's up with you?"

Amanda jumped, then turned to see Nolan on the grass at the end of the dock.

"Just enjoying the evening."

"Uh-huh." He came down the boards, then sat next to her. "So who's the new boyfriend?"

She scowled. Nolan was a born comedian who had a morning drive time radio program. Since most of his content was raunchy, a lot of people underestimated him. Amanda never had. Nolan was sharp. And he was good at reading people. Apparently, too good.

"The text you got. There was definitely a guy at the other end of the telecommunications highway."

"Not a boyfriend. Just a guy I'm seeing."

"So a hook-up?"

She grimaced. True, maybe. But it sounded so crass.

"Seeing. Going out." She paused, because they

actually didn't go out. They stayed in. But she didn't figure Nolan needed that detail. "Enjoying each other's company."

"Wild monkey sex?"

"Nolan!"

He chuckled. "Like I said. A hook-up."

"Whatever."

"For how long?"

"He lives in Dallas. We see each other when he comes to town."

"Again, I ask. For how long?"

"Fine. We met in July. But tomorrow's only our third date."

"Hmm."

She wasn't sure she liked the sound of that. "What?"

"Are you saying you don't like the guy?"

Her eyes went wide. "Hardly. He's great." More than great, if she was being honest.

"Then why are you trying so hard not to actually date him?"

"Shut up," she said, because she hated when her brother got the best of her. "And why is this even an issue for you?"

"I saw you after the last time you had a mysterious date, remember? About a month ago at The Fix?"

She nodded. It was the night that Derek had suggested a standing hook-up. And the night he'd invited her to stay. The offer had freaked her out, and she'd bolted. But it had also burned inside her, warming her up in ways that were incredible … and more than a little confusing.

She'd left his hotel room, walked the few short blocks to The Fix, and downed two Jalapeño Margaritas in quick succession. They'd taken the edge off the confusion, and for the remaining hours until closing, she'd hung out with her friends, laughing and joking and enjoying her memories of the night with Derek and her post-coital glow.

"What about it?" she asked.

"You seemed happy that night. A little off, too, but mostly happy. So I'm just wondering why if you like the guy, you're keeping him at arms-length."

"Like you're one to talk? You're not exactly Mr. Relationship."

"Maybe not. But right now, I'm not the center of the universe. You are."

She rolled her eyes. "Fine. And what makes you think it's me? Maybe it's him."

"Is it?"

She thought about it, but she honestly wasn't sure. Was he respecting her boundaries, or did he have boundaries of his own? And what did it matter, anyway?

"Dammit, Nolan, you're twisting this all up. We have fun. That's it. Drop it."

He hesitated, then nodded. "Okay." He kicked off his sandals, then sat on the dock next to her. For a minute, they both just kicked in the water. There was more he wanted to say, she was certain of it. But he kept quiet, and she loved him for it.

After a minute, she leaned over and shoulder-butted him. "Thanks."

"For what?"

"For being concerned about me. As brothers go, you're not too bad."

He laughed, then swung his arm around her. "Right back at you, sis."

———

HE'D DESTROYED HER, Amanda thought, as her body slowly came back together, every cell crackling with the fire of a spectacular orgasm.

"Wow," she said, even though that simple word

seemed far too difficult for her muddled brain to form.

"My sentiments exactly."

Smiling, she turned her head to find Derek laying beside her, propped up on one elbow. With his free hand, he was making slow, distracting circles on her breast. He matched her smile with a smug grin.

"You're setting the bar pretty high, you know," she teased. "How are you going to outdo yourself next time?"

His wide smile lit up his face. "I'm sure I'll find a way." He rolled her nipple gently between two fingers, and she drew in a tight breath, her body igniting all over again. "Mostly, I'm just happy to know that there's a next time on the agenda."

"Oh." She bit her lower lip, part of her wanting to pull away. The other part not wanting him to stop touching her.

"Amanda?"

What the hell was wrong with her? His mention of an agenda didn't amount to a proposal of marriage.

"Sorry. You're distracting me. And yeah, definitely more to come." She flashed him a flirty grin. "We have our standing hook-up, after all."

She leaned over and kissed him. "I should probably get going, though. If you're here on a Saturday, you must have work, and I—" She stopped when he took her hand and pulled her back toward him.

"I do, actually. But it's work you can help me with."

"Oh." She frowned. When he'd told her that he was a Winston, her first thought had been that he was exactly the kind of client she dreamed of cultivating. Someone with money and connections who could get her back on track career-wise. Because she'd gotten seriously derailed when she was with Leo.

Before Leo, she'd been on the fast track to getting not only her broker's license, but her certification as an international property specialist. One of the brokers in her office, Zeke, had offered to not only sponsor her, but to pass along his portfolio of domestic and international clients when he retired later that year. Plus, he was going to suggest that the company pay for all the courses required for international certification.

But then Leo had swooped in and Zeke had gotten into his head that she'd be more focused on her relationship than on her work. She'd been pissed, but she'd held her tongue. After all, she was in a great relationship, and so what if her career moved a little more slowly than she'd hoped?

She'd been an idiot, of course. Stupid for putting up with Zeke punishing her for having a life. And a total dufus for believing anything that Leo said.

When she finally picked herself up after the ground fell out from under her, Zeke had retired, he'd passed his portfolio off to one of the single men in the office (bastard!), and Leo was long gone.

Never. Again.

Never again would she let herself get that deep. She had too much to lose, and she'd learned her lesson with Leo when she'd sacrificed incredible career potential for a guy who didn't stick.

"Hey." Derek hooked his finger under her chin and tilted her head up so she was looking at him. "Where did I lose you?"

"Sorry. It's probably silly." She waited, but since he said nothing, she pressed on. "It's just that you must know that you're any real estate agent's dream. And when you told me who you are—well, I didn't want to cross a line."

She listened to her own words, amazed that they were true. Because as far as men were concerned, she'd never put up that wall. So why now? Why with him?

Because it's more than a hook-up?

She shoved the thought aside. She neither needed nor wanted a relationship. What they had was a good time and great sex. Which she enjoyed. A lot. Mixing in work might destroy the dynamic. That was all.

"If you'd rather not, I understand. But I'd really love the opinion of someone who knows the Austin real estate market. It's a commercial property, but in this case I don't think that matters."

"This case?"

His grin was mischievous, and she had the distinct feeling he was intentionally trying to reel her in. "The thing I want your opinion about."

She rolled her eyes. "Fine. You win. We'll go spend this lovely Saturday working."

He chuckled, looking more than a little smug. "I thought we could enjoy the day, too. Austin's the perfect temperature in September. Maybe take a walk, get some sunshine and exercise?"

"Exercise?" She slipped out of bed, then started to gather her clothes. "I think we just got one hell of an aerobic workout. And as for sunshine, there's always Vitamin D."

"Funny girl." He stalked from the bed to where she stood, then enveloped her in his arms, his naked body hard against hers. His body burned like a furnace, and she sighed with pleasure as the heat of him seeped through her.

"How about we take a shower and then get out of here. I'll scrub your back," he murmured as his hand drifted down to cup her sex. "I'll take care of the rest of you, too."

A moan slipped past her lips, and she nodded. "Mister, I think you have a deal."

Chapter Six

"IT'S COMPLETELY CHARMING," Amanda said as they stood across the street from the South Congress Motor Inn. "Or it will be once it's fixed up. Right now, it has great bones." She turned and flashed a bright smile at him. "I think you picked a winner."

He squeezed her hand, feeling ridiculously proud that she approved. "Thanks."

"I've lived in Austin my whole life, and I've barely given it a second glance. When will you be able to start renovations? For that matter, what are you planning to do?"

One by one, the bubbles of joy that had been floating inside him began to pop. "Actually, that's why I wanted you here today. I need to come up with a plan."

They went across the street to a new food truck court, then sat at a table and ate what probably qualified as the best brisket on the planet. And while they dug into the meat and coleslaw, he gave her a quick summary of his plan for the Winston Boutiques division ... and a summary of why it was currently on ice.

"So you want to start an offshoot of the hotel chain. Not the big, ornate fancy ones, but smaller places. Like high end boutiques."

"Right."

"I think that's brilliant."

"So do I," he said. "And the board was willing to consider my plan, at least until I hit a snag on this property. The owners originally said they were interested in selling. Now, they've got cold feet."

"So the Winston Corporation board is shutting you down because you may not be able to acquire this particular motel? That's silly. There are dozens of cute, retro motels in town. And gobzillions in Texas."

"Not disagreeing. But it's also not up to me."

She sat back with a sound of disgust that sent happy vibrations curling through him, simply from the knowledge that she was on his side.

"Maybe you should just do it yourself," she said.

"Screw the big corporate mentality and follow your grandfather's footsteps and do your own hotel."

"Great-grandfather, and it's a little more complicated than simply jumping in. But I appreciate the sentiment."

She scrunched up her mouth as if she was about to argue, then blew out a loud breath. "Okay, I suppose it would be. But how am I supposed to help?"

She'd finished eating, so he reached over and collected her trash, then tossed it with his in a trashcan at the end of their table. "Wanna walk? I'll explain while we window shop."

They were on the south end of the SoCo shopping area, which consisted of a stretch of South Congress Avenue about a mile past the river. Now they started walking north along the wide, charming street lined with funky shops. Everything from costumes to candy to original art to cowboy boots. On the horizon, the Capitol building loomed across the river. A long walk, but doable if someone was motivated.

Today, Derek wasn't. He only wanted to stroll lazily with Amanda, sharing his story and talking about whatever else came to mind.

"Okay, so tell me," she urged.

"The owners have run the place since they were in their twenties," he began. "And they're both in their seventies now."

"Any kids?"

"Nope."

She paused, and for a moment, he thought she was looking at the cute cat photos in the shop window. "I think you're wrong. No human kids, maybe, but after that much time, that motel is their baby."

"I know. That's the problem."

"What did you do? Offer them more money?"

"And we explained the concept of the boutique."

"Hmm. They still said no?"

He nodded, even though the question was obviously rhetorical.

"The thing is, they don't know if this is *Mary Poppins* or *The Hand that Rocks The Cradle*."

"Huh?"

"Okay, maybe not the best way of putting it, but in one, the nanny swoops in and makes everything magical and awesome. In the other, she comes in and people fall over dead. How do they know which one you are? Have you seen *Cradle*? Rebecca De Mornay sounds all sane and normal and awesome, but she turns out to be a basket case."

"I'll have to watch it," he said dryly as they began walking again. "But how does this apply to me?"

"Take them something concrete. I know a woman who does business remodels. She's helped on some of my properties that need a little work before we put them on the market. She could draw something up, maybe. Or walk through with the owners and tell them what you have in mind. That might be better." Her tone was musing, as if she was considering all the possibilities as they strolled. "More personal, you know."

He pulled her to a stop beside him. "You'd do that?"

"Sure."

"That would be fabulous," he said, and not just because he could use the help on the deal. No, the truth was he liked the idea that their lives were intertwining more and more. She'd snuck up on him, no doubt about that. And he still wasn't sure where they were going. But he was damn sure enjoying the journey.

"Her name's Brooke Hamlin. Do you want me to set up a meeting?"

"Yes," he said, then stole a quick kiss before she could protest that they were in public. "That would be great."

"AMANDA!" Brooke Hamlin flashed a picture-perfect grin and ushered Amanda and Derek into the recently remodeled detached office that dominated her tiny backyard. Tall and curvy, with blonde hair at least two shades darker than Amanda's, Brooke was the kind of woman who could easily appear on the cover of the *Sports Illustrated Swimsuit Issue*.

Today, her hair was pulled up in a messy ponytail, she had a streak of paint on her cheek, and she wore paint-splattered jeans and a SXSW tank top.

"Thanks so much for squeezing us in," Amanda said. "This is Derek Winston."

"Pleasure to meet you," Derek said, as they shook hands. "Like Amanda said, I appreciate you taking the time."

"Really not a problem. I've been refinishing a chest of drawers behind the office, so sorry about the totally unprofessional attire."

"Well, it is Saturday," Derek pointed out.

"True, but my business is still pretty new, and I'm always looking for clients, whenever they pop up. Or potential clients," she added with a grin. "And I'll always take the time to help a friend. So Amanda said that you're one of her real estate clients, and you have a problem with a commercial deal?"

Derek shot Amanda a quick glance before looking back at Brooke. "That's right."

Amanda exhaled. She'd made that client bit up on the fly. Just because it wasn't anyone's business, even a friend's, who she was dating.

Or, rather, sleeping with. They weren't dating. There was a difference, after all.

She realized with a start that Brooke was peering at her. "I'm sorry. What?"

"I said to come on over to the table. I've got some ideas."

The small office was dominated by a long oak table with a computer at one end, a huge monitor mounted on the wall above it, and a mishmash of blueprints, sample books, and brochures scattered over the tabletop.

"I did a little poking around since you called," Brooke said. "Take a look." She sat in front of her computer, but pointed them to the mounted screen. "I just put this setup in. Cool, huh?"

Amanda had to agree. The monitor flashed on and Amanda and Derek saw a photograph of the motel. "Since I didn't have any of your sketches," she told Derek, "I went a little wild."

The next slide showed the same motel, but cleaned up and modernized though still keeping the retro quality. "Quick and dirty," Brooke said, though Amanda thought it looked pristine and perfect.

"And I found a few images of the interior online. Here ... and here..." She tapped a few more keys and the same before and after shots came up of the lobby and a guest room.

"I didn't have time to do any mockups for the landscaping, but I found a property that has what I think would work great." The image flashed on screen. "And I also found a company that special-izes in copying old signage. That way you can keep the look of the old sign and update it with the Winston logo."

She sat back. "So that's pretty much all I had time to do, but—"

Amanda couldn't stop the laugh that bubbled out.

"What?"

"We called you barely thirty minutes ago."

A slight blush crept up Brooke's cheeks. "Well, I was intrigued. Once I got going, I couldn't stop."

"It's great," Amanda assured her. "Right?"

Derek nodded, looking a little shell-shocked. "More than great. It's incredible. I'd like to hire you to come with me to the meeting. Once I get it set up, maybe we could put together a video proposal."

"Use some morphing software to show the transformation? Yeah, that sounds great."

They exchanged numbers and made plans to be in touch, and Amanda sat back feeling more than a little smug.

"What?" Derek said once they were in the car.

"I don't know. Usually I'm at the center of a deal. It was fun to watch you two work."

"She's talented."

"She really is," Amanda agreed.

He leaned over to the passenger seat and kissed her. "So are you."

"Watch it," she chided. "She might see."

"Would that be so bad?"

Amanda shrugged, not entirely sure how to answer that. "She'd know I was lying. I practically said you were only a client. Which, actually, was also a lie."

"It doesn't have to be."

His tone had changed from teasing to serious, and she studied him as he concentrated on backing out of the driveway. When they were back on Riverside Drive, she asked him what he meant.

"I want to buy a condo. And I need a real estate agent who can narrow down potential properties when I'm not around. Funny thing is, I could only think of one person I want to work with."

"Seriously? Here?"

"This is your market, right?"

"Well, yes. But why? Are you moving here?"

He shook his head, and though Amanda knew she should be relieved, she could feel a tiny knot of disappointment forming in her gut.

"Since the boutique division may be dead in the water, I'm taking over as the director of North American operations."

"Sounds important."

He grinned. "It's not shabby. But it involves a lot of travel. I already have a place in Dallas, Los Angeles, New York, and Chicago. I want one here, too. The room we've been using is a corporate room, so I can't leave personal things there."

She nodded, thinking how nice it must be to just buy a condo wherever you needed one. "Well, I'm happy to help." She meant it, too. She'd thought it would be weird to seek out work, but having Derek hand it to her on a platter was something entirely different.

"I thought maybe you could scope out the market then shoot me some possibilities. I'm thinking a two bedroom, two bath. Even if I don't keep it, that's better for resale than a studio."

"You got it. Budget?"

"I only poked around a bit into the Austin market, but I think a cap of three mil should work?"

"I can find you something exceptional for that. And probably for significantly less if we keep our eyes open."

"Fair enough. You keep your eyes on the market, and I'll keep mine on you."

She caught herself smiling. "That's a plan I can live with."

With a sigh, she leaned back, enjoying the drive. They'd decided to take advantage of the rest of the day and stroll through the botanical gardens, and it took no time at all for them to reach Zilker Park. Soon they were walking among the greenery, and when Derek took her hand, Amanda didn't protest.

She did, however, start thinking about those other towns. Those other condos. And as they approached the Japanese garden, she pulled her hand away and shoved it into her pocket.

"So you've got condos all over the place already? How come? You're just now getting this new North American job, right?"

He glanced at her, but she couldn't see his eyes behind his sunglasses. "My work has always required a lot of travel. But I don't actually own all of the properties. The Chicago one is my mother's, although she's never there. Mellie and I share it."

That had to be a relative, but even so, a green-tinted demon poked her in the gut, forcing her to blurt out the words and make a fool of herself. "Who's Mellie?"

Now his mouth twitched, and she was certain he was reading her mind. "My sister."

"Oh." She really should Google this man.

"Anything else you want to ask me?"

"No. Yes." *Shit.* "I was just wondering if there were other girls like me. I mean, how many cities have Winston Hotels with corporate rooms?"

Had she really said that? If it were possible, she'd

knock that damn demon to the ground and crush him dead under the heel of her sneaker.

"Ah, the answer to that would be all of them."

She swallowed.

"They all have corporate use rooms." He took her hand and tugged her to a stop in the shade. "But there are no other women. Not in hotel rooms or my apartment or anywhere else."

"Oh." An unreasonable amount of relief flooded her. "Okay. I was just curious."

"Curious? Or jealous?"

She licked her lips, then focused on the floral pattern of her shoes. "Maybe a little of both."

"Interesting," he said, and when she looked back up, he was smiling.

"Do you know what I think we should do?" he asked.

"What?"

He bent forward, then whispered the words, his mouth so close that his lips brushed her ear, making her shiver. "I think we should go back to the hotel so that I can prove to you that you have absolutely no reason at all to be jealous."

Her breath left her in a woosh, and she nodded. "Yeah," she finally managed. "That sounds like a great idea to me."

Chapter Seven

SOMETHING SHIFTED BENEATH HER, and Amanda bolted upright, gasping and confused. She had no memory of what she'd been dreaming, but she understood what had awakened her. Derek had rolled over, and her head must have slid off his chest and onto the mattress.

She allowed herself a satisfied smile as she recalled the way he'd kissed his way all over her body, leaving her warm and tingly. And then, when he'd moved on to kiss between her legs, not letting up until she'd come three times, well, then she'd done more than tingle.

He'd refused to let her return the favor. Instead, he'd pulled her close, and she'd fallen asleep tucked up against him. Now, though, it was time to come back to reality.

With a loud exhale, she shook herself, trying to erase the grogginess. She ran her hand through her hair, caught a glimpse of the clock, and sighed.

Past ten.

Part of her wanted to snuggle back under the covers and go to sleep. But the part that was still sane and remembered her no strings, no relationship commitment told her to get her ass out of bed and go home.

Stupid sane part…

She dragged herself to the bathroom, quietly gathering clothes along the way, careful not to disturb Derek, who looked like he could sleep for a year. Only when she was inside the small room did she flip on the light and get dressed.

A few minutes later, she cast one quick glance back to Derek, then dragged herself out of the room. The door closed with a soft *snick*, and she grimaced, hoping it didn't wake him. She knew he was tired; she was tired for the same reason.

The thought made her smile, and she hurried toward the elevator, leaning against the wall until the doors open, and she could step out into the lobby. Her sneakers made no noise on the tile floor, and she kept her head down, startled when she heard a deep voice calling, "Amanda?"

She turned and saw Easton Wallace, tall and chiseled, pushing himself up out of an overstuffed leather chair in the lobby bar.

"Easton!" She hurried forward, accepting his hug. "I haven't seen you in months. What have you been up to?"

"I was in LA for a while. Saw Jenna out there. Depositions and a huge document production." He shook his head, like a dog shaking off fleas. "Thank God that's over."

"Why are you here alone?"

"I was with a date, but she got called into work. She's a surgeon," he added, in response to her questioning look.

She glanced at the two glasses on the table where he'd been sitting, and he laughed. "Scotch for me, cranberry juice for her." He indicated the abandoned chair. "We'd just ordered some chips and guacamole. Want to join me and catch up? I can get you something other than her discarded juice."

She hesitated, feeling strangely guilty about sitting with another man while Derek was asleep upstairs. Especially Easton. Not that there was anything between them now, but they'd gone out a few months ago. But it wasn't serious—Amanda didn't do serious—and they'd become good friends. And Easton still fed her potential clients.

Amanda was pretty sure that Jenna was convinced they'd slept together, and Amanda hadn't bother to correct her. Jenna was convinced Amanda was nursing deep scars after Leo and that getting involved with other men would act as a healing balm. Jenna was probably right. Not that Amanda would ever admit that out loud.

"So what are you doing here?" he asked, after the waiter had delivered the chips, and Easton had ordered her a drink. "Hot date?"

"I was visiting a friend," she said primly.

"Uh-huh. Let me guess, you've got some new guy on the hook, and you're about to lure him into buying a million dollar property."

"You asshole." She shot the insult at him as a joke—and she knew perfectly well that he was joking, too. But it hit a little too close to home. She was about to hook Derek up with a condo. And she was sleeping with him. True, she'd purposefully not gone there when they'd first met, but now…

"Kidding." He put his hands up in supplication.

"Change of subject. How's Jenna seem to you?" From her own conversations, Amanda was worried that Jenna missed Texas too much.

"She seemed iffy on the job. I don't think it's quite what she expected. But I'm sure she'll rally."

Amanda sighed and nodded, and they continued in that vein for a while, discussing mutual friends, movies, and other random topics. When Amanda had finished her drink, she put the glass down and started to stand. "It's been great catching up, but I really should get home. I need to—"

Derek.

He was standing right across the lobby, his eyes fixed on her, his expression unreadable.

Nausea crested, and her stomach flipped over. "I—"

But she couldn't manage anymore.

"Amanda?" Easton stood, and when she didn't move, he turned to look the same direction. A second later, he turned back to Amanda. "Who is that?"

The question pulled Amanda back to herself. "I'm sorry. I have to go." She snatched up her purse and walked as fast as she could toward Derek, but he saw her coming and moved to the elevator. She was only a few feet away when he stepped onto a car, then turned to face her.

She started get on, too, but he held out a hand, his palm flat. A virtual wall between them.

"Derek, it's not—"

But she didn't get to finish. The doors closed, and he was gone.

She gulped in air, telling herself he was the one being an ass. She hadn't done anything wrong. She was just talking to a friend.

Besides, they had no commitment. Had made no promises.

All true.

So why did she feel so guilty?

SHE COULDN'T SLEEP, and at one in the morning she finally gave in, and grabbed her phone, intending to send him a text.

But when she opened the app, she saw there was already a message waiting—several, actually—and she realized that the phone had switched to DND mode after eleven.

Derek - I'm sorry. I should have stayed and talked. I was an ass. Let me know if you need more of an apology.

Derek - A pox be upon my soul.

Derek - *May the fleas of 10000 camels infest my armpits.*

Tears filled Amanda's eyes, but they were the good kind. Relief and laughter all rolled together.

Amanda - Trying to decide if I should say something or see how this escalates.

Derek - About to try plagues of Israel. Save me.

Amanda - I'm sorry, too.

Derek - No need. You didn't do anything. (Did you?)

Derek - Ignore that. Our deal was no commitment. None of my business.

Amanda typed out her response—*is that what you want?*—then erased it before hitting send.

Amanda - Bumped into an old friend. His date ran out on him. We caught up.

Derek - wipes brow in relief.

Amanda - So we're good?

She cringed the second she pressed send. The question sounded far too needy. But there was no calling it back. Too bad she didn't live in another age. With a letter she could have hightailed it to her mailbox and pulled back the envelope.

But of course they were good. That was pretty much the point of the whole text conversation.

But if they were good, why wasn't he responding?

Frowning, she closed the app and re-opened it, then checked her signal strength. All good.

Damn.

She was about to power off her phone—at least then she wouldn't know he was actively ignoring her—when the doorbell rang.

She glanced at her watch, considered ignoring it, then felt her phone buzz in her hand.

Derek - Knock Knock

Grinning, she hurried to the door and flung it open. "Who's there?"

"An asshole?"

She shook her head as she ushered him in. "No. Definitely not. How did you find me?" She realized for the first time that she'd never given him her address.

"We corporate big shots have all sorts of under-handed methods to find people."

"Uh-huh. Well, however you managed, I'm glad you did." She drew in a breath, and asked the lingering question. "We're good, right? We'll see each other again next month?"

"Actually, no."

"We're not good?" A shock of panic cut through her. "But—"

He took her hands. "We won't see each other next month. I'll be in Europe all of October."

"Oh." The weight of her disappointment surprised her. She licked her lips. "This isn't a brush-off, is it?"

His smile was gentle. "Did you not read all my groveling texts? Honestly, it's going to be a pain. Twenty hotels in twenty-five days. Pity me."

"Maybe when you get back I'll have found the perfect condo for you to relax in and shake off all that European dust."

He took a step closer. "I hope so."

Suddenly, she was very aware of her own breathing. "Um, so when will you be back?"

"The Tuesday before Thanksgiving. Will you be in town or traveling?"

"I'll be here." She grinned. "That's what I'll be thankful for." Had she really just said that? It was true, but had she really said it?

From the breadth of his smile, she supposed that she had.

"Good. It's a date. Or, I guess, since we're not dating, it's a non-date."

"Absolutely," she said, with a perfectly straight face. "Non-date."

He took a step back toward the door. "About earlier, I know we said no promises."

"We did."

"And no commitments."

She nodded.

"I still didn't like it," he said. "Seeing you with another man."

She licked her lips, her pulse strong in her neck. "And I felt guilty when I saw you, which is crazy since I didn't do anything but hang out with a friend."

"You know, considering all of that, it really sounds like we're dating."

She lifted a shoulder, trying to appear casual when she felt anything but. "And sometimes generic tastes like the real thing. But it's not."

He studied her, then nodded slowly. "Fair enough." He bent forward and kissed her cheek. And as he did, he whispered to her. "Just keep in mind, sometimes, generic is better."

Chapter Eight

CONSIDERING he was thousands of miles away, Amanda managed to stay more in touch with Derek than she did with most of her friends. They sent text messages—including a few that probably qualified as sexts—talked on the phone, Skyped so they could see each other, and even exchanged a few emails.

Amanda told herself that this was all because they were working hard to find him a condo. He'd told her that if she found the right property, he'd close sight-unseen so long as she was happy with it. His trust had humbled her—and the potential commission had kept her working long hours.

After five weeks, though, she'd finally found the perfect place. A two-bedroom penthouse condo with a corner view of the river, a private deck and infinity pool, and security out the wazoo. As a bonus, the condo came furnished, and the previous owner had excellent taste. The contemporary-style furniture both accented the lines and angles of the glass and steel condo, and had the benefit of being comfortable.

Despite the contemporary design and decoration, the overall impression was of comfort. Bottom line, it felt like a home.

True to his word, he'd looked over the pictures, negotiated the price, and then asked her if he should pull the trigger. When she'd said yes, he'd made a cash offer, and seventeen days later they'd closed on the property. The owners were in Hawaii, the buyer in Prague, and the real estate agent in BookPeople, Austin's biggest independent bookstore, where she was buying up every magazine she thought might interest Derek so that she could make the place even more homey.

And, of course, she'd bought new sheets for the bed.

Now he was due back in Austin and she couldn't stop fussing. She'd paced the length and breadth of the condo at least nine times, checked on the congratulatory cake she had in the refrigerator, rearranged the flowers in the entry hall, and generally made herself crazy fussing and worrying.

Mostly, she was looking forward to seeing him.

Not to mention new sheets for the bed.

Finally, she heard ding from the security system that signaled someone accessing the elevator to the penthouse. She hurried to open the champagne, poured two glasses, and then parked herself in front of the door. A few moments later, the front door beeped with the code she'd texted him. She hurried to the door, then greeted him with the drink.

"This is fabulous," he said, his eyes only on her.

"You haven't even looked around."

He bent and kissed her. "I'm not talking about the condo."

She felt her cheeks flush, more pleased by his words than she ought to be. To hide her reaction, she lifted her glass. "To new homes."

"To new beginnings," he countered, his eyes never leaving hers as they took a sip.

"Um, you should change the code on the door," she said as she lead him toward the kitchen.

"Why? Who knows it?"

"Well, I do."

"Anyone else?"

She shook her head.

"Then it's fine."

"It's random," she said. "You should pick numbers that you can remember."

"You mean something other than the day we met?"

She froze. She'd done that on a whim, not thinking for a moment that he'd realize what the numbers represented, too. Casually, she tossed a smile over her shoulder. "Is it? What a coincidence."

"Uh-huh." He reached for her hand, then tugged her to him, then picked her up and flung her over his shoulder while she squealed and pounded on his back.

"Put me down!"

"Not until you admit that date's important. One for the history books. A real red letter day."

"Dammit, Derek." She kicked, but he held on tight.

"Nope? Okay, guess I'll have to give myself the tour. I'm thinking I'll start in the bedroom."

"Put. Me. Down."

"Yes, Ma'am." He bent over and dumped her onto the bed. Before she had a chance to recover, he was on top of her, caging her in with his hands and his legs. "Admit it."

She shook her head, fighting laughter.

"I'll get the truth out of you one way or another."

"What ways?"

"I could tickle you."

She shook her head. "I'm a kicker. You might lose something important."

"Spank you?"

She met his eyes, saw heat reflected back. "I take the Fifth."

He held her gaze a bit longer, the moment heavy with possibility. Then a slow smile crossed his face. "I'm thinking maybe this."

Slowly, so that she had time to anticipate the kiss, he lowered himself to her.

They made love slowly, no wild rush of lust. No struggle to get free of clothes and shoes. This felt like a deeper passion. A burning need. A coming together.

It was real and tender and a little terrifying.

But Amanda wanted it. Had been longing for it all the time he was gone. To come together not out of wild lust, but out of the need to be together, as fully and completely as possible.

The realization that she'd been craving that scared her, and she didn't share it with him. But when he took her to the edge—when his body pushed hers over into the stars—she whispered one thing for him to keep with him.

"I missed you," she said, then let herself explode in his arms.

———

AMANDA DIDN'T REMEMBER FALLING asleep, but by the time she woke up, the sun was streaming in through the open curtains and Derek's alarm was blaring.

Derek, miraculously, was sleeping through it.

"Hey," she shook his shoulder. "Your alarm."

Nothing.

"Don't you have a plane to catch?"

That did it, and he rolled over, the heel of his hand pressed to his forehead. "Sorry. Had a late night last night." He aimed a wicked grin her direction. "Oh, wait. You look familiar…"

She smacked him with her pillow. "Get dressed and I'll drive you to the airport before I go to my parents."

"Right. Is there coffee?"

She laughed, realizing this was the first morning they'd shared. Usually, she crept back to her place before dawn. Apparently, Derek was slow to come alive.

"There will be," she promised, then left him to finishing his crawl into the land of the living.

A few minutes later, he came into the kitchen. "I like this."

"The kitchen?"

"The way you look in the kitchen."

She raised a brow, but he just shrugged, not in the least chastised.

"Why aren't you dressed?" She let her eyes roam over him, noting that he looked just as appealing all rumpled in the morning as he did when he was tailored and polished for work.

"My flight's grounded," he said. "Engine trouble. And all the commercial flights are booked. My assistant has me out on an early morning flight, so I'll still get back to the ranch in time for Thanksgiving." He shrugged. "That's okay. I can enjoy my new condo."

"I'm sorry. Weren't you going to see your sister today?" He'd mentioned a couple of times that he hadn't seen Mellie in a few months, since she'd been working at the Winston Hotel in Australia.

"I'll see her tomorrow."

"Still…"

She held her mug in two hands and regarded him thoughtfully. "It sucks to be alone. Why don't you come to my parents' house and have Thanksgiving with us?"

"That's tomorrow."

She shook her head. "Not in my family. Thursdays we always spend at a center for underprivileged kids with learning disabilities. We started volunteering a few years ago, and it's become a tradition."

"So today's your family's Thanksgiving? I don't want to intrude."

She waved away the words. "Oh, please. It'll just be us, my mom and dad, and my brother. But we usually have a good time. Although I warn you that Nolan takes some getting used to."

A moment ticked by, then another, and still he didn't say anything. All he did was look at her, as if memorizing her face.

"Um, Derek? Look, if you don't want to—"

"I'd love it." The words seem to burst out of him.

"Really?"

"Yeah," he said, the sincerity in his voice unmistakable. "Really."

DEREK HADN'T BEEN nervous visiting a girl's parents' house since high school, but he couldn't deny that he'd been nervous the entire time that they'd been in the car from downtown to Amanda's family home. Those nerves had kicked up even higher during the walk to the door.

And then, finally, he'd gone into jittery overdrive during that small span of time before he and Amanda finally stepped into the house and he met Huey and Martha Franklin, along with Amanda's stepbrother, Nolan.

From that moment on, he wasn't nervous at all.

Amanda had introduced him as a client—though Derek wasn't entirely sure any of the three believed that. Notwithstanding, they didn't press for details. Instead, they pampered him. Inviting him to sit and watch football with Huey and Nolan while Amanda and Martha set the table. And providing him with ample beer to take the edge off.

"Beware my brother," Amanda said before she disappeared into the kitchen. "Just because someone pays him to make an ass of himself on the radio, he thinks he's funny."

"Nonsense," Nolan said. "Mostly I think it's funny that they pay. Ba-dum-ching."

She rolled her eyes. "Lame. If you're going to riff when my friends are here, at least be clever."

He shot her the finger.

"Nolan," Huey said, in the kind of tone one used with a twelve year old.

Nolan and Amanda caught each other's eyes and snickered, while Derek watched Amanda, and realized he couldn't wait for her to meet Mellie. Probably not the best thought to have considering her no-relationship policy. But she'd also coded his door with their pseudo-anniversary. And she'd invited him to her parents' house for Thanksgiving.

Maybe not conclusive proof that there was something growing between them, but pretty damn close.

He'd slowly been sneaking up on it, but watching her now, he couldn't deny that he wanted that. Not her, but *that*. The shared family. The realness. The closeness.

He wanted a relationship and all that came with it.

And even if she wasn't admitting it out loud yet, he was certain Amanda wanted that too.

"All right, you two," Martha said, bustling into

the living room and aiming her daughter toward the kitchen.

"We're all about gender roles here," Amanda quipped. "Go. Be manly and watch football."

"She hates football, and she loves hanging with Mom in the kitchen," Nolan told Derek. "She only pretends to be put out."

"I heard that," Amanda called from the kitchen, and Nolan winked at Derek conspiratorially.

At half-time, Nolan took him to see the dock which, considering it was about as average as a dock could be, Derek assumed this was so that Nolan could play the role of protective sibling. When Nolan told him flat-out that if Derek hurt his sister, he'd figure out a way to have him flayed on social media, Derek knew he'd been right.

"Let's hope it doesn't come to that," he said dryly.

"Don't hurt my sister, and it won't. She's been through more than enough hell with that prick Leo. She doesn't need any more of that shit."

"I'd sooner cut off my own arm than hurt her," Derek said, filing away the name Leo for future reference.

"That can be arranged, you know," Nolan said.

Derek laughed. "You're almost as funny in person as you are on the radio."

Nolan's eyes widened. "You listen to my show?"

"Whenever I can."

"Well, shit, man." He clapped Derek on the back. "Forget everything I said. You're practically one of the family."

Amanda's voice carried from across the yard, interrupting them. "What are you guys up to?"

The guys looked at each other, then back to Amanda with equally innocent expressions.

"Not much," Nolan said. "Just telling my buddy Derek here to be good to you."

"Sweet thought," she said as she got closer. "But did you miss the part where we're just friends?"

"Oh, you mean the bullshit you told mom and dad? Yeah, I missed that." He waggled his eyebrows. Watching her, Derek couldn't decide if she was amused or exasperated.

Finally, she rolled her eyes at Derek. "Ignore him," she said. "He's a first class asshole."

"Maybe," Nolan said, flashing his cockiest grin. "But he's a smart one."

Chapter Nine

"WHERE ARE YOU TODAY?" Amanda asked the second she answered the phone.

Derek grinned, loving the way she just dove into a conversation. "What, no hello?"

"Hellos start conversations that end in good-byes. And with all of your traveling with this job, I feel like we're saying way too many goodbyes."

He couldn't argue with that. "Disneyworld, actually. The Winston family of hotels is about to break ground for a glorious resort. Complete with shuttle service to the land of the mouse."

"Sweet. Nice to do business in the happiest place on earth. Or is that Disneyland?"

"Neither as far as I'm concerned. Not unless you're with me. And even if you were tempted to jump a plane to Orlando, I'm leaving tomorrow for St. Louis."

"I think it's snowing there. You have a coat, right?"

"I pack for all occasions now," he said, which was true. Though he loved that she worried. The truth was, he was getting damn tired of living out of a suitcase. And if some of the corporate changes that were in the works got pushed through—which they should for the good of the company—then he'd probably be traveling at least seven more days each month.

Prestigious job. Crappy situation.

And except for the two meetings he'd had with Brooke at the motel, that project was moving slowly. Now, at least, the ball was in the owners' court. Derek and Brooke had made their pitch. Now they just had to wait.

"Any chance you'll be in Austin for New Year's Eve? I know we're not technically dating, but there was this dress that I just couldn't resist, and so I bought it. I was kind of hoping you'd have the chance to see it."

With every word, his heart seemed to flip over and die.

"You have no idea how much I wish I could."

"Really? You can't?" The disappointment in her voice both broke his heart and lifted his spirits. "I saw an article about a huge New Year's Eve bash at the Winston. I thought maybe you could come down as, you know, the official representative of the Winston family."

"That's a great idea," he told her. "Unfortunately, it's not original."

"What do you mean?"

"We hold those events at every Winston hotel in the country. I'll be at the one in Chicago as the corporate rep. Unfortunately, New Year's Eve is a workday for me."

"No problem. I knew it was a long shot."

"I'm glad you thought of it, though." He pitched his voice low. "That means a lot."

"Oh. Well. You know."

He could picture her cheeks, flush with the embarrassment of being caught out. And her disappointment that he couldn't join her tugged at his heart.

"You should definitely go to the party, though. It's always fun. Good food. Great music."

"I don't know. I—"

"I'll reserve a VIP table for you. If you don't use it, that's fine. But it would be a shame to waste a dress. Maybe take Brooke. You two could make it a girl's night. Or Nolan."

"Maybe."

"Just don't take a date," he said, and was rewarded with her laugh.

"Deal."

"And one more thing."

"Yeah?"

"Send me a picture from the party. I want to see you in your dress, especially if I don't get to see you out of it."

"Yeah," she said softly. "I will."

When they hung up, he was smiling. Which took the edge off the mile-high pile of paperwork he still had to go through. He'd managed to make a small dent when the phone rang again. He snatched it up, expecting Amanda, only find that the caller was Jared.

"Hey buddy, happy almost New Year."

"I'd say the same, but it's all a load of bullshit, isn't it?"

"Not exactly in the holiday spirit, are you?" Derek asked. "What's wrong?"

"Same bullshit as always. I'm on a damn hamster wheel. So are you, my friend. That job for Daddy? You're going nowhere fast. Unless you consider flying all over the United States going somewhere."

Derek leaned back in his chair. "How much have you had to drink?"

"Not enough."

"Got a date for New Year's Eve?"

"Did. Don't anymore."

Now was not the time for a lecture on either Jared's work ethic or his relationships. "So come to Chicago. I'm playing host, so you'll be on your own, but so what?" And unlike Amanda, Jared knew enough of the attendees that he would be fine without Derek.

"I don't know. Maybe. Shoot me a ticket, okay?"

"Will do."

Jared's heavy sigh filled the silence. "Why are we doing all of this?" Jared asked.

"All of what?"

"Exactly," Jared said. And then he hung up.

AMANDA ALMOST DIDN'T GO to the New Year's Eve gala at the Austin Winston Hotel. What was the point without Derek there, too?

In the end, though, she decided to go for four reasons. First, he'd told her to, and he'd taken the trouble to get her a VIP table. Second, he'd asked for pictures of her in the dress, and what was the point of putting it on to take a picture if you didn't actually go somewhere? Third, she actually wanted to wear the dress, and a gala was the perfect venue. It wasn't as if a full-skirted black and white ball gown would be appropriate for showing a three-bedroom, two-bath condo overlooking the river.

Mostly, though, she wanted to be close to Derek. Although that emotion scared her to death. She'd put so much into the relationship with Leo, and when it fell apart she'd been ruined for months. Emotionally and in her career.

Maybe she was being stupid to let herself get in deep with Derek, but she told herself it was safe because it was essentially a monthly thing. A moving hook-up. Friends with Ultra Benefits. And that was okay.

That's what she told herself.

But on nights like tonight, she just wanted him. And if she couldn't be with him, then being in the hotel that bore his name would have to do.

"What do you think?" she asked Reece, twirling for him in The Fix. Since the bar was hosting its own celebration tonight, it was overflowing with patrons, and Amanda appreciated Reece taking the time out to humor her.

"You look amazing," he said, and she curtsied.

"Thank you, kind sir."

Honestly, he was right. She *did* look amazing, and she'd saved two pictures of the getting dressed process to her phone. She'd already texted the first one to Derek—her in a lacy bra, matching panties, a garter, and stockings. After all, why not start from the bottom up?

He'd texted back that it was cruel of her to torture him, and she'd continued to get dressed with a huge smile stretched across her face.

The second picture was as she looked now. She'd put her hair up, so that only a few tendrils fell around her shoulders, leaving the elegant neckline on full display. As for the dress itself, the bodice was fitted and zipped up the back. The material was white, but not blinding. A simple belt of grosgrain ribbon separated the form-fitting bodice from the flared skirt made of layers and layers of material.

The dress was a rare splurge, and it made her feel as lovely as Grace Kelly. Too bad Derek wasn't there to see her. But she did send him the second picture of her in the dress, too.

Now she just needed to get one more picture of her actually at the gala. Even if she left early, she'd be able to show him that she was there.

And, honestly, even with her friends there as well, she wasn't sure she could stay until midnight. That might be a little too depressing.

"You're not walking over, are you?" Reece asked.

She shook her head. "Nolan's actually getting us one of the carriages, so that should be fun."

Reece laughed. "You'll look like Cinderella."

"Speaking of, have you talked to Jenna? Last time I did, she was still looking for work after the mess with that horrible company she went to work for in LA."

"This morning," Reece said. "Terrible time of year to be looking for work."

He looked so worried about her that Amanda wished she hadn't brought it up. "She'll be fine. She's so freaking talented and—oh, there's Nolan."

Reece waved her off. "Go. Have fun in the glitz and glam. We'll be here with jeans and boots and beer."

"Don't bullshit me. This place has the best cocktails in the city."

"We do indeed," he said as she hurried through

the door, then let her stepbrother help her into the carriage.

"Very cool idea," she admitted.

"I have them every once in a while," he said. "And I figured you'd need cheering up, what with your boyfriend being absent and all."

"He's not my boyfriend."

"Uh-huh. Pull the other one, why don't you?"

She rolled her eyes, but didn't otherwise protest. He might not be right about the label, but she did want Derek there.

It didn't take long to reach the hotel, and once they were in the ballroom, Nolan went off to mingle. "This place is dripping with fodder for the show. I brought a notepad and a recorder." He patted his pockets. "I'm set."

She laughed, then waved him off. Then stood like a dolt wondering what to do next. She'd just noticed Brooke on the far side of the dance floor when Martin Arand came up beside her. They'd never been good friends, but she knew his name and face well enough. He was the man Zeke had entrusted with his portfolio. And the man Zeke had sponsored for a brokership.

He was the man who'd stolen her life, and all because she'd let Leo steal her heart. Bastard.

She wiped the frown off her face, then smiled up at the man. "Martin. How lovely to see you."

"I saw you here and just wanted to say hello. I know you still haven't gotten your broker's license. If you ever need a sponsor, just give me a call."

Her smile was ice. "That's so nice of you. Thanks."

"Of course, of course. Any time," he said. She resisted the urge to punch him—it was Zeke's fault, not Martin's—and the evening went on.

He had, however, reminded her of her priority. With Derek not there, she might as well network.

She'd met a few of the owners in Derek's building and that had led her to other potential clients, many of whom were here. So she mingled and chatted and flirted when necessary. But it all felt hollow and useless.

She didn't want to schmooze clients. She wanted—

Well, no, it didn't matter, because Chicago was a long, long way away.

She headed to her VIP table to leave a note for Nolan and Brooke. She'd had her fill of the gala extravaganza, and simply wanted to go home.

But, of course, she had no pen, so she turned around to search down a waiter.

There he was.

Which made no sense because he was in Chicago. But that was him, no doubt about it. And she wanted to run to him—but that would make a scene. Plus, she'd probably fall. Her shoes weren't exactly made for running.

So she waited, breathless, for him to come to her.

"Hey, beautiful. That dress looks amazing on you."

"You're only saying that because I want to hear it."

"And because it's true."

Her grin spread so wide it hurt.

"I liked your pictures."

"Did you?"

"Mmm," he said, then stepped closer.

"How are you here?"

He lifted a shoulder. "I told the office that I was taking New Year's Eve off."

"That simple?"

He shook his head. "No. But that important."

Tears pricked her eyes. "Thank you."

He brushed his thumb over her lower lip, the sensation hinting at a kiss.

She swallowed. "What do you want to do?"

"I've come a long way to get here. Right now, I just want to hold you. Dance with me?"

With a nod, she slid into his arms. "Thank you."

"For what?"

"This has been the best night ever."

His brow rose. "Has been? It's not over yet."

"I know. But I didn't want to forget to tell you."

She rested her head against his chest as they swayed to the music. "And I already know this is one of those rare, triple gold star evenings."

Chapter Ten

THERE WAS nothing about spring in Austin that Amanda didn't like, especially this year. She'd seen Derek at least once each month since New Year's Eve, the bluebonnets that covered the state were stunning, and Jenna was back from LA.

"I know I keep saying it," Amanda said to Jenna as they sat at a table by the window in The Fix, "but I'm just so ridiculously happy you're back. Even if the reason does suck."

Jenna had moved to LA a while back to take a job with a marketing company. That whole situation had been a massive fail, and now she was back. A fact that made Amanda positively giddy.

"It did suck," Jenna admitted, taking a sip of her Loaded Corona, a specialty at The Fix and one of Jenna's favorites. "I ended up broke and coming home with my tail between my legs."

"You came home," Amanda said, leaning over to put her hand on Jenna's. "That's the important part. Besides, look at you now. A partner in The Fix and doing the exact job you wanted to do. Marketing and Event Planning. I think you must have some pretty good karma clinging to you, my friend."

At that, Jenna smiled. "It is pretty cool. And completely unexpected. I still can't believe it."

"Can't believe what? That Reece and Brent would pull you in? The three of you are like the planets, the sun, and the space between. A unit, you know? Of course they wanted you in. Especially when they need you to do the marketing. That's not their thing—Reece is all about management and Brent's deal is security—and it's sure not Tyree's."

Tyree Johnson was the original owner of The Fix on Sixth. And Amanda felt like a complete idiot for not realizing that the place was in financial trouble. But apparently it was—and continued to be—because even though Tyree had taken on three partners in Jenna, Brent, and Reece, he'd still publicly announced that unless The Fix was firmly in the black come New

Year's Eve, then he'd sell the place. And Amanda knew the market well enough to know that the most likely buyer was Bodacious, a corporate chain bar that not only had an infantile business model, but also served truly crappy food and watered down drinks.

Brent and Reece had bought into the partnership, providing working capital for the rest of the year. And Jenna had come in on her skills alone. But she'd already proved her worth as far as Amanda was concerned. "The Man of the Month contest really is brilliant," she told Jenna. "And it was all your idea. Although I think I provided some wisp of inspiration."

The competition centered around hot men vying for a slot in a calendar. Which mean that soon there would be shirtless men on stage. Which meant more women in the bar. And that meant more drinks sold.

Ergo, the brilliance.

Jenna laughed. "I just hope I can pull it off."

The contest was still in the planning stages, with the first competition a few weeks away. "It'll be a huge success. You'll see."

She leaned back in her seat, then took a sip of her Jalapeño Margarita. "And the rest?"

Jenna's eyes widened. "What rest?"

"You and Reece. You're really going to tell me nothing's going on?"

Jenna rolled her eyes. "Yes. I'm really going to tell you that. He's my best friend. Since childhood. End of story."

"Uh-huh."

"Please drop it."

"Fine." Amanda had pulled that thread before, and she'd undoubtedly pull it again. She could let it go for now.

"How about you?" Jenna countered. "You're dating someone, aren't you?"

"Oh, please. No." Amanda fought the urge to cross her fingers under the table. "You know me better than that."

"Yup, I do. And you haven't been talking about your conquests nearly as much since I got back. So, what? Do you have a guy tucked away in your attic somewhere?"

"Actually, yes. I take him out and dust him off about once a month."

"I'm serious," Jenna said.

Amanda blinked at her friend, the picture of innocence. "And you think I'm not?"

"Fine. Whatever." She finished her drink. "Another?"

"Sure," Amanda said. For a second, she thought about telling Jenna the real truth. About the man whose presence she craved. Who made her feel special and even loved.

But she didn't. The feelings were true, but they were scary. And acting on them meant change. And right now, between her and Derek, she didn't want anything to change at all.

"IT'S BEEN way too long since we've gotten together," Derek said, his eyes meeting Landon's in the locker room mirror. They'd just finished a killer game of squash, and they were both dripping with sweat. "Hell of a game, though."

"Right on both counts." Detective Landon Ware and Derek had been having drinks at The Fix On Sixth the night that he met Amanda. They'd met when Landon was working in the Dallas Police Department ten years before and had been assigned to investigate a suspicious death in one of the Dallas Winston Hotel's rooms. Murder, it turned out. A wife who'd poisoned the engraved water bottle her husband took with him to work, because she was certain he was having an affair. She was right. And the husband and the mistress had died in the penthouse.

"You're still seeing that cute girl you were checking out last year?"

He nodded. "Hard to believe it's been that long."

"Time flies," Landon said. "You two must be serious." Landon was a strong man, and he looked it. Not huge, but a solid block of muscle, covered by a layer of tattooed, black skin. But he had exceptionally kind eyes, and it was Derek's theory that the combination was what made him such a great detective. Everybody talked when Landon was in the interrogation room.

Just like Derek was talking now. "I think we are. Hard to know."

"Is it? I haven't really dated much—not since that shit with Vanessa—but I seem to recall the question being a little more clear cut."

"I'm pretty sure nothing is clear cut where women are concerned." He sat on the bench and pulled on his shoes. "I'm out of here. I'm actually meeting her in an hour. A work free Saturday for both of us."

"Give me a call when she doesn't have you tied

down." Landon winked, then tossed his locker key and caught it. "We'll have a rematch."

"You got it."

Derek showered and was out of the gym in record time. He waved to the owner, Matthew Herrington, then stepped out into a gorgeous spring day. He headed down Congress toward his condo, pausing only when he saw a familiar face coming toward him.

It took him a second, but he finally recognized the tall man with dark hair and movie star looks. "Parker? Parker Manning."

He saw the confusion on Parker's face, then the recognition as Parker shook his head in surprise. "I almost didn't recognize you," Derek said. "It's been, what? Ten years?"

"About that. I'm not even sure where I saw you last."

"Something to do with our parents, I'm sure."

Both Parker and Derek came from families with Texas money that was sunk deep. The Manning family with their oil and gas roots, and the Winston family with ranching and the hotel chain. And despite popular opinion, the high roller club in Texas wasn't overflowing with members. Most anyone with that kind of portfolio knew everyone else, and Parker and Derek had spent many afternoons together at country clubs and other watering holes for old Texas money.

"Are you living here now?" Derek asked Parker. "I thought I'd heard you were in LA."

"Was. Just moved to Austin. Well," he amended, "my company's been here for awhile, but I just made the move myself."

As he spoke, he was looking over Derek's shoulder, and he took one long step to the right, which put him behind Derek. Then he slipped into the shadows of a nearby building's entrance alcove.

"Problem?"

Parker shook his head. "I know that woman."

Derek glanced over his shoulder at a woman with long dark hair and cat's eye glasses, then looked back at Parker. "Bad breakup?"

"Not exactly. Let's just say I want to stay off her radar for awhile. I think she needs some space," he added, obviously in response to Derek's questioning expression.

"Looks like you've become quite the gentleman."

Parker's lips twitched. "It happens. So what's up with you?"

"Work. Travel. I did just close a deal to

purchase a small motel to renovate." The owners of the South Congress Motor Inn had finally accepted the offer, and Derek couldn't wait to get the Winston Boutiques division up and running.

His phone rang, and he frowned when he saw that it was his assistant. "I need to take this. It's either an emergency or I'm going to have words with my assistant." She knew he preferred text or email on the weekends. Calls were strictly for crises.

"No problem. We'll catch up soon."

"Absolutely," Derek said, then connected the call. "Elizabeth? You know it's Saturday."

"I'm so sorry, Mr. Winston. But Mr. Ingram's father just called. He wanted you to know that Jared tried to commit suicide."

IT TOOK a few hours and a half dozen calls, but Derek finally managed to piece the story together. His friend had tried to OD on pills, and he was currently in a private hospital in Vermont for recuperation and psychiatric evaluation.

Derek was scheduled to fly up there first thing in the morning.

Now, he stretched out on the couch, not doing a

damn thing except waiting. Not for tomorrow, but for Amanda. She was due any minute, and though his first instinct had been to cancel their date, he hadn't done so. He'd kept silent because the only thing that he was certain about in this crazy day was that she was the person he wanted to see.

A moment later, he heard the keypad beep. She entered, started to flash her bright smile at him, then faltered.

"Derek? What's wrong?"

Immediately, a wave of guilt crested over him. He hadn't cancelled the date because he wanted to see her. But did he really have the right to bring her down, too?

"It's fine," he said, pushing himself up onto his elbows. "I should have called. I'm not really good company today. I don't want to ruin your Saturday, too."

"Hmm." She dropped her purse on the entry table, then came to kneel in front of him. She reached over and felt his head. "You don't have a fever."

"It's not that." He took her hand, deciding he should tell her. "Jared tried to kill himself."

She froze. "Your friend? The one you told me about from boarding school?"

He nodded.

"Oh, God. Derek, I'm so sorry."

"I don't want to lay this on you, too. You should just go. I can—"

"No," she said, her voice firm. "Now scoot over."

He didn't have the motivation to argue, so he scooted.

She slid onto the couch next to him, then pulled his head down against her. "Do you want to talk about it?"

"Not really. He's a good friend, and I love him, and part of me thinks I should have seen it coming."

"It's not your fault."

"I know that, too."

Their eyes met, and the concern he saw on her face made him feel cherished. He wished Jared could have felt that way.

"There is one thing."

"Whatever you need."

"I'm so tired."

"Well, then close your eyes and go to sleep."

"Will you stay?"

"Derek, yes. Of course. I'm not going anywhere."

"Thank you."

"Shhh," she murmured, stroking his hair. "Just close your eyes and drift."

And so he did, trying to wrap his mind around the entire day. But he couldn't. All he could process was the fact of Amanda. He'd tried to push her away. She'd stayed anyway.

Now here she was, when he was raw and exposed. Shattered and confused. Basically a mess.

And all he could think was, thank God.

Chapter Eleven

EVEN IN UPSTATE NEW YORK, July was a bitch, and Derek wiped sweat from the back of his neck as he and Jared walked the grounds at the hospital.

In the months since Jared had tried to kill himself, Derek had made the trip at least a half-dozen times, squeezing the visits in between his increasingly busy travel schedule for work and his regular trips to Austin, which in Derek's mind had become both sacred and frustrating.

Sacred because he cherished his days with her.

Frustrating because even after a year, they were still flying under the radar. They were in a *de facto* relationship—any lawyer would say so—but she still refused to describe it that way. Or do anything to move it forward.

But that wasn't a problem for today.

Usually, when Derek visited Jared, they took a walk, then played some chess, then talked about something utterly mundane. Last time, they'd actually debated the lighting design in *Citizen Kane*, a conversation all the more interesting since Derek knew nothing about film. Neither did Jared, really, but under the circumstances, Derek didn't push that point.

In other words, their conversation to date had been safe. Dull. Even boring. And definitely not insightful.

Today, Derek had asked his friend *why*.

"A lot of reasons," Jared said. "Some I'd just gotten mixed up in my head. Some Dr. Crowley says I may not fully understand. But I guess the bottom line is that I couldn't figure out how to get off the damn hamster wheel. I mean, you know my life. What was the point?"

"I think you're the point," Derek said, and Jared lifted a shoulder. And, thankfully, smiled.

"Yeah, maybe so. But I've got a ways to go before I find my way back to a version of me that I want to hang out with, you know?"

"I think I do. You staying here for a while, then?"

Jared nodded. "Another three weeks. About

time I put myself in the shop for maintenance, don't you think?"

Derek had to laugh, relieved that some things didn't change. "Yes. Past time. I've been worried about you."

"I know. I'm sorry about that."

"Don't be. I get it."

Jared studied him for a minute. "Do you?"

"Yeah." He frowned. "Why?"

Jared waved the question away. "Spend too much time around shrinks and you start thinking like one. I just worry about your hamster wheel, you know? May not be as rickety as mine was, but it's still spinning."

He thought of Amanda. And he thought of the unending crisscross pattern he was following over the continent, and the renovations on the motel that were stalling because he didn't have a free second to push the project forward.

He thought of all that, and he nodded. "Yeah. I know."

WHEN AMANDA GOT to The Fix Wednesday night, she was surprised by how crowded it was.

This was the sixth of the bi-weekly Man of the Month contests—they'd kicked off in April—and each one had drawn a bigger crowd.

"Amanda!"

Amanda turned just in time to get caught up in Megan Clark's exuberant hug. A makeup artist by trade, Megan had recently begun working with Jenna, and had come up with an advertising flyer that seemed to be working.

"You know," Amanda said, "I think this may be the best night yet. Your flyers definitely upped the interest, and what's on the flyer's not too bad either. I mean, Parker? Holy hell, that man is hot." Somehow Megan had convinced Parker Manning —*the* Parker Manning—to enter the contest. And Amanda could only wonder what sort of bribe she'd used to make *that* happen.

Griffin Draper had come in with Megan, and now he rolled his eyes. An up-and-coming voice actor and web series creator, Griffin was extremely talented, but also self-conscious of the scars he'd received after being burned as a child. Megan, Amanda knew, had become one of his closest friends.

Megan ignored Griff's reaction, pushed a lock

of dark hair off her forehead, and nodded in solidarity with Amanda. "Seriously hot," she agreed.

"Honestly, if this were a bachelor auction instead of a calendar contest, I think I'd have to bid." Amanda started to fan herself, but when Megan clapped a hand over her mouth in an obvious attempt to hold back laughter, she turned around—only to have her eyes fly open at the sight behind her.

Parker was there, yeah. But she wasn't embarrassed by what he might have overheard. For one thing, it was true, and he was surely used to being fawned over by women by now. For another, she barely even registered Parker.

No, what had her eyes going wide was the man *with* Parker—*Derek*. What on earth was he doing there tonight?

She heard the others talking, but she was too shocked to process words, so she didn't clue back into the conversation until Megan spoke up. "Who's your friend?"

"Sorry," Parker said. "Everyone, this is Derek Winston."

Everyone started introducing themselves and shaking hands. And then it was Amanda's turn. She met his eyes, and she knew hers were full of questions. Some of her friends who came to The Fix knew they were acquainted, of course. But Brooke wasn't around at the moment, and so right now it just seemed easier to take his extended hand, ignore the ever-present zing of connection, and mutter her name in introduction.

She was certain that everyone could read her face and figure out what was going on, but no one seemed to notice her at all.

"You're Winston Hotels, right?" Griffin asked. "Nice properties."

"Thanks," Derek says. "It's a family business, but I've taken over as the director of North American operations. I'm in town visiting the Austin properties. Since Parker and I go way back, I thought I'd come watch him shake his groove thing up on that stage."

"If my groove thing does any shaking it won't be on that stage," he said. And although it might have been Amanda's imagination, she could have sworn he looked at Megan.

"There you are!" Taylor D'Angelo hurried forward, her ponytail bouncing. She shoved her way through the crowd, then grabbed Parker's arm. "You're supposed to be in the back. It's almost time for the show to start."

"See you all later," Parker said as he was dragged away.

About the same time, Megan headed toward the stage, leaving Derek and Amanda alone, with Amanda gaping at the man. She was trying to gather her thoughts, when a familiar looking man approached, and she remembered him as the guy sharing a table with Derek that very first night they met.

"Hey," the man said, "I didn't expect to see you here."

"I came to see Parker humiliate himself."

"Didn't we all? I'm Landon, by the way," he added, thrusting his hand out for Amanda. "An old friend of Derek's."

"Oh. Right. Well, I'll leave you two to talk. It was great to meet you."

She saw Derek's eyes go wide, but she didn't hesitate. Just cut through the crowd and headed to the back of the bar. In all the time they'd been together, they'd never come to The Fix. They'd never talked about it; it seemed to be an unspoken rule.

So to see him here now was strangely upsetting. No, she thought. Not upsetting. It was confusing. Because as much as she'd wanted some time to think, she also couldn't deny an almost overpowering urge to sit with him at a table in the back, their heads bent close together as they watched the contest. And that desire—that craving to have more of him than she already had—had been growing constantly for months.

And, yeah, that scared her.

Frustrated, she dragged her fingers through her hair. Bottom line, she wanted Derek. Heavy underscore beneath the bottom line? She wanted all the parameters tailored to her convenience.

Well, hell.

Fortunately, he hadn't pushed her to change the status quo. And surely tonight was just a coincidence.

In fact, he was probably just as surprised as she was, which accounted for whatever odd vibe she'd picked up.

Biting back a grin, she eased toward the back of the bar. If she slipped out through the back exit to the alley while the contest was going on, no one but Derek would miss her. And he'd undoubtedly know to look for her at his condo.

She eased through the crowd and was just about to slip into the hallway, when she heard the familiar voice calling her name.

"Amanda."

She turned, her breath leaving her as she saw him, his broad shoulders filling the space and his eyes full of so much passion she knew that her panties were already soaked. If it wouldn't be so damn dangerous, she'd just drag him into the ladies room and have her way with him right then.

Instead, she just smiled and said, "Hey. I'm sorry for cutting out on your friend. I was surprised to see you. I was afraid he'd read something on my face."

"Baby, that's not even on the radar. I just want you to meet me in our room in an hour. Will you do that for me?"

"Absolutely," she said, although she was surprised that he wanted to meet at the hotel. Usually they went to the condo. Then again, they had met in July. Maybe he wanted to celebrate their anniversary month in the same room they'd managed so well in before.

"I have news," he said. "I was going to wait to tell you, but baby, I'm too excited."

"Really?" She couldn't imagine what it could be. Maybe tickets to a show tonight? They'd been talking about going to see something this summer.

He took her hand, then leaned in close, his

breath tickling her ear. "I'm moving permanently to the condo. And I'm cutting out the work travel, too. No more waiting. From now on, you can have me anytime you want me." He pulled back just enough to meet her eyes. "And baby, I always want you."

Chapter Twelve

DEREK HAD KNOWN that his news was going to blow her mind, and he'd debated whether to drag out the news or tell it in one fell swoop. In the end, he'd decided to do both. Tell her about the move to Austin first, and then tell her the rest when he got her alone.

What he hadn't expected was such a visceral reaction from her. But here she was in their hotel room, pacing back and forth, barely saying a word.

"I guess I don't understand," she said. "You just decided to up and quit your job?"

"My job that required me to travel so much, yes. I'll still be employed." At least, he hoped so. That discussion was part of the dragging it out portion of tonight's program, and right then she didn't look primed to hear it.

"But—"

"Amanda, please. Sit down."

She scowled, but complied, settling herself on the foot on the sofa in the suite's living room. Since he wanted to see her face, he sat on the ottoman across from her. "I did a lot of thinking after Jared's suicide attempt," he began, then tried to put into words for her how much he'd empathized with Jared's feeling of his life having no meaning, no real connections.

He took her hands then. "But I'm not Jared. I have you. And I wanted more, but that wasn't possible unless I made some changes. I thought— hoped—that you wanted me in your life. And not just in a way that pops in periodically."

She swallowed, but she didn't hesitate. And when she said, "Yes, of course I do," he thought those were the sweetest words in the world.

"Jared described it as a hamster wheel, and he's right. There's only one way off, and that's to make the jump. Take a leap."

"A leap of faith," she said, her voice fragile. "At least you're luckier than a lot of people. You have your money and your family business. A safety net for if you fall."

"True," he said. And not true, though he didn't

tell her that yet. No sense muddying things up before they needed to be.

He drew in a breath and continued. "But here's the thing. It's not just that I'm sick of traveling, it's that I want to see you more. And not just more often, but *more*. Richer. Deeper. I love what we have, don't misunderstand. But I don't want to be going in a circle on a hamster wheel with you. I want a highway. Or long, lazy country roads. I want a horizon and a future."

"You want a relationship."

"Yes. No. I think we *have* a relationship. I want to put the stamp of approval on it and trot it out for our friends and family to see."

She pressed her lips together. "What if I'm not ready for that?"

He leaned forward so that he could put his hands on her knees. "Baby, why wouldn't you be? What is it that's scaring you?"

She drew in a breath. "I don't know."

He slid off the ottoman so that he was on the floor looking up at her. "I think you do. I talked to Nolan, and Leo was a prick. He left without warning, he was an asshole. And that makes you scared. But I'm not Leo. You're going to have to put up a fight to get rid of me."

Her eyes met his, and for a moment, he saw their future in her soul. Then she hugged herself and shook her head.

"Dammit, Amanda, you're scared to take a risk on something just because it might fail. That puts you on the damn hamster wheel."

"Forget the fucking hamsters," she snapped. "And you know what? It's not just me. Or have you forgotten about the motor inn. Because that's some pretty risky business, but I haven't seen you going after that project in almost a year."

"Right, well, that's something else I wanted to tell you. I took that leap, too."

She blinked at him, then slowly sat down. "What?"

"The motel's just been sitting there, waiting to be renovated. My pet project going ignored, and I couldn't stand it. So Since the board didn't want it to be a division, so I set up my own corporation—DW Boutiques. The Winston Corporation is coming in as an investor, which is how I'm capitalizing it. But it's all on me. This fails, my name in this business is shit. My dad will probably stick me back in the mailroom."

Fire lit her eyes, and his heart swelled. "Derek, that's amazing. Congratulations."

"I can't do that, though," she continued, and he felt that flicker of hope fade into ash. "I don't have a safety net."

"Sure you do. You have me." He grinned. "I'll need a good real estate agent."

"That's only the net for if the business fails." A tear trickled down her cheek. "The truth is, I didn't even love Leo. It was my ego that was hurt, and my business, which really pissed me off. But if I go all in and then I lose you…"

She stood and started pacing. Again. And, dammit, he let his frustration get the better of him.

"For Christ's sake, Amanda, I love you. I love you enough to take a risk. To go out into the world with you at my side and to tell people that we belong together. That we're in this whole thing together, hamster wheel or highway. Don't you get it, baby? For me, it's all about you. I do," he whispered. "I really do love you."

Tears streamed down her face, and she hugged herself so tight her knuckles were white.

"Maybe I don't love you."

He shook his head. "That one's lame," he said. "I know you do."

A strangled laugh bubbled out of her. "Yes," she

said simply. "I do." She licked her lips. "But maybe that's not what matters. I'm sorry, Derek," she blurted as she hurried for the door. "I really am, but I have to go."

Chapter Thirteen

"I WANT HIM," Amanda said to Jenna as they sat in the back office of The Fix, just before the lunch crowd came in. Amanda had spent over twenty-four hours doing nothing but watching sappy movies and drinking wine, and contrary to pop culture, she hadn't figured a single thing out.

"I mean, I really do want him. I was even getting there on my own. And then he went and dumped everything on me without warning. I wasn't ready. But maybe I was on my way to getting ready."

"So tell him that."

Amanda sighed. "I thought I did. But I think he heard *no.*"

And honestly, maybe she'd said no. He was mixing up the idea of a relationship—and the way he was describing it as a long highway all the way over the horizon sounded a whole lot like 'til death do us part. And to go from not even telling their friends—until this very moment—to side-by-side burial plots was a little too zero to sixty for her.

Or maybe she was just making excuses.

"Why am I making excuses?" she asked. "I mean, if I'm really ready—if I love him the way I'm supposed to—wouldn't I be ready to jump right in?"

Jenna shook her head. "Reece was full of excuses. But we're great now. Maybe you're just scared."

"I am," Amanda said. "I really am. That it won't work out. That my business will fail."

"Fail? Why?"

"I—" She threw up her hands. Because the truth was that she hadn't cocktailed her way to a lead or a client since she met Derek, and yet she had more clients than ever simply from the folks she'd met in his building.

"Oh, hell." Tears trickled down her face and she felt like an idiot. "If I never say yes, I can't be wrong."

Jenna frowned. "What?"

"That's it. I think that's what's holding me

back." She twisted a strand of hair. "I thought I loved Leo—it wasn't love. It was lust. But they seemed the same at the time. I thought everything was fine, and then he just left. Boom. Everything I believed was wrong."

"So you're saying that maybe what you believe about Derek is wrong, too?"

Amanda exhaled slowly. "What if he realizes he doesn't love me after all? I mean, obviously I'm a basket case. Maybe he bolts."

"Maybe he sticks."

"How can I be sure?"

Jenna lifted a shoulder. "You can't. So the question is, are you willing to take the chance?"

Amanda nodded, thinking about Jenna's words. Maybe Jenna was right and you really couldn't know. But who could ever really know anything? So she had to focus on what she *did* know. That Derek had been there for her since that very first day. That he loved her. He respected her. She wasn't just window dressing the way she'd sometimes felt with Leo.

Derek *saw* her. He respected her and her boundaries. He supported her hopes and helped launch her dreams. He was present in the world with her.

She frowned. Maybe that was love. Seeing and sticking.

Amanda started to suggest that to Jenna, but Tiffany Russell, one of the waitresses, burst into the room. "Oh! Sorry! I didn't mean to interrupt, but I was looking for you," she said to Jenna. "Here are Taylor's keys. She said you wanted to borrow her car. I've been using it while mine's in the shop, but I don't need it today."

"Thank you. Reece has the Volvo and I just need to make a quick run to Costco."

"Need help?" Amanda asked.

"I've got it. But thanks. You okay?"

"Much better. You're amazing."

"Love you," Jenna said.

"Right back at you."

PARKER TOOK A SIP OF SCOTCH. "I think it boils down to the fact that women are weird."

"Cheers to that," Derek said, lifting his glass to toast with Parker and Landon. On the other side of the bar, the bartender, Eric, looked across the room at a pretty waitress who was clearing glasses. "I'm guessing you agree?" Derek asked, but Eric just muttered something about side work and hurried down the bar.

"So what do I do, gentlemen?" Derek asked.

"Do you love her?" Landon tossed back the dregs of his bourbon.

"Yeah. Not even a doubt."

"Then you stick," Parker said. "What else can you do?"

"Run for your life," Landon quipped.

"My friend in law enforcement has a calloused heart," Derek explained to Parker. "And unfortunately, I think I have to stick. She's holding my heart. Run, and I'd rip the damn thing right out. Pretty sure I need one, too."

"I'm cutting you off, Pretty Boy," Landon said. "You're getting way too poetic. Or pathetic." He frowned. "Or are those the same?"

"If you're sticking, tell her. Maybe that's all she needs to hear," Parker said. "If she knows she can't get rid of you, maybe she figures she'll just put up with you."

"Nice," Derek retorted.

"Where is she, anyway?"

Derek lifted a shoulder, then let it fall. "No idea." He blew out a loud breath. "All I want is for her to get her shit together and realize that the two of us together is a good thing. Is that too much to ask?"

"Not in my book." Landon managed to slur all the words. "But women are weird. That's mostly why I'm done with them."

"I should call her, right?" Derek looked at Parker, because Landon was less than useful. "Or should I not call her and give her space?"

Parker shook his head. "I never read the rule-book on those. Not sure you—"

SCREEEEEEEEEEECH!!!

The horrific sound of tires slamming and metal crunching filled the bar, followed almost immediately by the wail of multiple car sirens.

There weren't many people in the bar at lunchtime, but those that were bolted for the door, with Landon leading the charge, stone-cold sober now. "Call 911," he yelled to Derek. "Tell them we need an ambulance, and fast."

"Who's hurt?" Derek asked, waiting for the call to connect, but Landon was already out the door.

Parker, however, was at the window. "I'll get Reece," he said. "It's Jenna."

"*What?*" The cry from behind them came from Tiffany, who was now racing to the door. Amanda was pacing her, but as she passed Derek, she shot him such a pitiful look he almost hung up on 911 just so he could go comfort her.

"Yes," he said in reply to the dispatcher. He ran through all the answers, gave all the necessary information, then hung up and pushed outside into the noise of the crowd.

As soon as he was through the door, Amanda threw herself into his arms. He hugged her tight, but his mind was only half on her. He was looking at the car. At Jenna's slumped form. At the hole in the back window that didn't look like it could have come from an accident.

Landon was at the driver's side beside her, and Tiffany was standing by pacing, holding her cellphone, and telling anyone nearby that she was on the phone with Taylor and there was supposed to be airbags. Why were there no airbags?

Soon, the wail of sirens filled the street, and at the same time, Reece came running, so fast he looked to be flying. He pushed through the onlookers, his face a mask of terror, then knelt beside her just as the first paramedic arrived on the scene.

Landon backed away then, consulted with the second paramedic, then finally came over to where Derek stood with his arm around Amanda.

"They think she's going to be fine. They're

taking her in just to be sure, but I think everything will be okay."

"I think she's pregnant," Amanda said. "She hasn't said anything, but——"

"She is," Landon said. "She told the paramedics. That's another reason they're taking her in. Just to be safe."

Amanda nodded, not sure if she should be relieved or worried.

"One other thing—someone threw a brick through the back window. That's what made her lose control."

"What?"

"Who would do that?" Derek asked.

"No idea. But I'm going to ask around. Try to learn if anyone saw something." He looked between the two of them. "Maybe you two should go home."

"Maybe we should," Derek said once Landon was out of earshot. "Do you want to come home with me?"

"No," Amanda said, the word making his heart break a little more. "I mean yes. But I need to tell you something first."

"Wha——"

But he didn't get to finish because she silenced

him with a kiss, long and deep and overflowing with passion. "I love you," she said when she pulled away. "More important, I know you love me, too. And I've figured out what that means. It means you're here. With me. Beside me, like for always. Right?"

He nodded, her words making his legs a little weak. "Nowhere else, baby."

"That's what I want." She nodded toward the ambulance. "Not the wreck. But what the two of them have. Reece and Jenna. And My parents. And my brother now that he's found Shelby. And I think that's you, Derek." She licked her lips. "The man who'll always be beside me. I think it is. Honestly, I'm sure it is."

"Baby..." He took her hand, wanting to kiss her, but she was still talking.

"I'm sorry I was scared. Or stupid. Or both. But I love you." She sniffled. "I think I thought by being an ostrich I could keep myself safe." She nodded at the wreckage. "But you can't do it."

"No, you can't."

"Yeah, well, if I'm going to navigate all these long dark scary roads you keep talking about, then I want someone strong by my side. I pick you," she said.

"Well, that works out great. Because I picked you a long time ago."

———

"SAY IT AGAIN," Amanda begged as Derek thrust deep inside her. It was still early, but they'd spent the rest of the afternoon in bed making love. Fast and hard. Slow and lazy. Didn't matter. They just wanted each other.

"Say it," she begged.

"I love you," Derek murmured as he buried himself inside her. "I love you, Amanda. And I always will."

"I love you, too," she said, but that was all she could manage, because he was close, and he'd quickened his pace, thrusting deeper each time until he'd completely filled her, and she didn't know where he ended and she began.

"Touch yourself," he demanded. "Come with me."

With a moan, she slid her hand between their bodies, then stroked her clit, her passion rising as she felt his muscles tense. And then—faster than she'd anticipated—her body went over. Her sex clenched with the force of the orgasm, milking him.

Taking him to the final, utter edge until they both fell, shattered and satisfied, against each other as the world slowly put itself back together.

"That was spectacular," Amanda murmured.

"You're spectacular."

She smiled, but didn't roll over. She was too wiped to even move.

Or so she thought until the phone rang. Then she leaped for it, saying a silent prayer when she saw it was Reece. "How is she?"

"Perfect," he said. "And so is the baby."

"Thank goodness." She nodded to Derek, and gave him a thumbs-up.

"Jenna said she has a favor to ask Derek, and that surely he won't turn down an injured pregnant woman."

"What's that?"

"One of the contestants dropped out of the next Man of the Month contest. She wants him to take the slot."

Amanda let her eyes drift over the naked man beside her, then decided that she was generous enough to share his bare chest with the world. So long as there was no touching. "He's in," she said, flashing him an evil grin.

"Shouldn't you ask him?"

"Nope," she said, scampering backward as Derek tried to grab the phone. "He told me he loved me and that he'd do anything for me. I'm calling in my marker. Wait!" she cried as Derek stole the phone, and the last thing she heard was the echo of Reece's laughter.

———

JUST SHY OF two weeks later, she stood in the crowd at The Fix on Sixth and watched the crowd ooh and ahhh over her shirtless, gorgeous boyfriend.

"They do know he's mine," she asked Jenna, who was still using a crutch, but otherwise fine.

"They know."

Amanda nodded with satisfaction. "I knew he was going to win, you know."

"Oh? How?"

Amanda shrugged. "Simple. He's been my man of the month for the last year. About time he got the title to go with it."

Then she blew a kiss to the man she loved, and sighed with pleasure when he caught it and sent it right back, his eyes on no woman but her.

Epilogue

"YOU EITHER LET me check out the apartment, or you come sleep at my house. Your choice." Landon stared down the girl. And considering their ten year age difference, he needed to continue thinking of her as *the girl*. "I'm not taking risks with you. Brent would have my ass if something happened to you."

"Brent's not the boss of me." Taylor pushed back her hair as she shrugged, and Landon knew damn well she was trying to act disaffected. But she was spooked.

Hell, considering everything that had gone on in the last week, she'd be an idiot not to be spooked. First her car with Jenna driving. Now the disturbing notes. And then to come home to find the apartment unlocked. Maybe she'd left it that way … but he wasn't going to let it slide without checking every inch.

He put a hand on her shoulder, and felt her stiffen beneath his palm. Immediately, he regretted the action. He'd felt the chemistry between them the first moment they'd met when she'd barreled into him on Sixth Street, almost knocking him over.

It was that chemistry that had almost kept him from taking this assignment.

And it was that chemistry that had convinced him to go for it.

Bottom line, he didn't trust anyone else to keep her safe. So he was on her. Twenty-four hours a day. Just not *on* her.

"Wait here," he said, then moved slowly through the place, his weapon at the ready just in case. He checked each room, each closet, each nook and cranny. *Nothing.*

"Taylor?"

"I'm here. I'm good. But can you—*ah!*"

He was back by her side in an instant. "What?"

He'd left her by the closed front door, and he arced the gun, covering the full interior. Nothing.

"Maybe you imagined it?"

But even as he asked it, a small tabby cat leaped from the top of the refrigerator, making Landon step forward to get out of its way—and Taylor to jump toward him, obviously not realizing the threat was only a cat.

She ended up in his arms, her soft body pressed against his. Her curves welcome after so long a dry spell. He told himself no. He told himself all the reasons it would be a bad idea. He told himself he was a fool and an idiot and that he'd regret it in the morning.

All of the words pounded through him. But so did the heat of her body. So did the rise and fall of her chest.

"Landon." His name on her lips sounded like sin.

That was it. That was all it took for him to push every scruple aside. To break every rule he'd set for himself. And with one violent action, he pulled her tight against him, bent his head, and captured her mouth with his.

Are you eager to learn which Man of the Month book features which sexy hero? Here's a handy list!

Down On Me - meet Reece
Hold On Tight - meet Spencer
Need You Now - meet Cameron
Start Me Up - meet Nolan
Get It On - meet Tyree
In Your Eyes - meet Parker
Turn Me On - meet Derek
Shake It Up - meet Landon
All Night Long - meet Easton
In Too Deep - meet Matthew
Light My Fire - meet Griffin
Walk The Line - meet Brent
&
Bar Bites: A Man of the Month Cookbook

Down On Me excerpt
_____

Did you miss book one in the Man of the Month series?
Here's an excerpt from Down On Me!

Chapter One

Reece Walker ran his palms over the slick, soapy
ass of the woman in his arms and knew that he was
going straight to hell.

Not because he'd slept with a woman he barely
knew. Not because he'd enticed her into bed with a
series of well-timed bourbons and particularly
inventive half-truths. Not even because he'd lied to
his best friend Brent about why Reece couldn't drive
with him to the airport to pick up Jenna, the third
player in their trifecta of lifelong friendship.

No, Reece was staring at the fiery pit because he

was a lame, horny asshole without the balls to tell the naked beauty standing in the shower with him that she wasn't the woman he'd been thinking about for the last four hours.

And if that wasn't one of the pathways to hell, it damn sure ought to be.

He let out a sigh of frustration, and Megan tilted her head, one eyebrow rising in question as she slid her hand down to stroke his cock, which was demonstrating no guilt whatsoever about the whole going to hell issue. "Am I boring you?"

"Hardly." That, at least, was the truth. He felt like a prick, yes. But he was a well-satisfied one. "I was just thinking that you're beautiful."

She smiled, looking both shy and pleased—and Reece felt even more like a heel. What the devil was wrong with him? She *was* beautiful. And hot and funny and easy to talk to. Not to mention good in bed.

But she wasn't Jenna, which was a ridiculous comparison. Because Megan qualified as fair game, whereas Jenna was one of his two best friends. She trusted him. Loved him. And despite the way his cock perked up at the thought of doing all sorts of delicious things with her in bed, Reece knew damn well that would never happen. No way was he risking their friendship. Besides, Jenna didn't love him like that. Never had, never would.

And that—plus about a billion more reasons—meant that Jenna was entirely off-limits.

Too bad his vivid imagination hadn't yet gotten the memo.

Fuck it.

He tightened his grip, squeezing Megan's perfect rear. "Forget the shower," he murmured. "I'm taking you back to bed." He needed this. Wild. Hot. Demanding. And dirty enough to keep him from thinking.

Hell, he'd scorch the earth if that's what it took to burn Jenna from his mind—and he'd leave Megan limp, whimpering, and very, very satisfied. His guilt. Her pleasure. At least it would be a win for one of them.

And who knows? Maybe he'd manage to fuck the fantasies of his best friend right out of his head.

It didn't work.

Reece sprawled on his back, eyes closed, as Megan's gentle fingers traced the intricate outline of the tattoos inked across his pecs and down his arms. Her touch was warm and tender, in stark contrast to the way he'd just fucked her—a little too wild, a little too hard, as if he were fighting a battle, not making love.

Well, that was true, wasn't it?

But it was a battle he'd lost. Victory would have brought oblivion. Yet here he was, a naked woman beside him, and his thoughts still on Jenna, as wild and intense and impossible as they'd been since that night eight months ago when the earth had shifted beneath him, and he'd let himself look at her as a woman and not as a friend.

One breathtaking, transformative night, and Jenna didn't even realize it. And he'd be damned if he'd ever let her figure it out.

Beside him, Megan continued her exploration, one fingertip tracing the outline of a star. "No names? No wife or girlfriend's initials hidden in the design?"

He turned his head sharply, and she burst out laughing.

"Oh, don't look at me like that." She pulled the sheet up to cover her breasts as she rose to her knees beside him. "I'm just making conversation. No hidden agenda at all. Believe me, the last thing I'm interested in is a relationship." She scooted away, then sat on the edge of the bed, giving him an enticing view of her bare back. "I don't even do overnights."

As if to prove her point, she bent over, grabbed her bra off the floor, and started getting dressed.

"Then that's one more thing we have in common." He pushed himself up, rested his back against the headboard, and enjoyed the view as she wiggled into her jeans.

"Good," she said, with such force that he knew she meant it, and for a moment he wondered what had soured her on relationships.

As for himself, he hadn't soured so much as fizzled. He'd had a few serious girlfriends over the years, but it never worked out. No matter how good it started, invariably the relationship crumbled. Eventually, he had to acknowledge that he simply wasn't relationship material. But that didn't mean he was a monk, the last eight months notwithstanding.

She put on her blouse and glanced around, then slipped her feet into her shoes. Taking the hint, he got up and pulled on his jeans and T-shirt. "Yes?" he asked, noticing the way she was eying him speculatively.

"The truth is, I was starting to think you might be in a relationship."

"What? Why?"

She shrugged. "You were so quiet there for a while, I wondered if maybe I'd misjudged you. I thought you might be married and feeling guilty."

Guilty.

The word rattled around in his head, and he groaned. "Yeah, you could say that."

"Oh, *hell*. Seriously?"

"No," he said hurriedly. "Not that. I'm not cheating on my non-existent wife. I wouldn't. Not ever." Not in small part because Reece wouldn't ever have a wife since he thought the institution of marriage was a crock, but he didn't see the need to explain that to Megan.

"But as for guilt?" he continued. "Yeah, tonight I've got that in spades."

She relaxed slightly. "Hmm. Well, sorry about the guilt, but I'm glad about the rest. I have rules, and I consider myself a good judge of character. It makes me cranky when I'm wrong."

"Wouldn't want to make you cranky."

"Oh, you really wouldn't. I can be a total bitch." She sat on the edge of the bed and watched as he tugged on his boots. "But if you're not hiding a wife in your attic, what are you feeling guilty about? I assure you, if it has anything to do with my satisfaction, you needn't feel guilty at all." She flashed a mischievous grin, and he couldn't help but smile back. He hadn't invited a woman into his bed for eight long months. At least he'd had the good fortune to pick one he actually liked.

"It's just that I'm a crappy friend," he admitted.

"I doubt that's true."

"Oh, it is," he assured her as he tucked his wallet into his back pocket. The irony, of course, was that as far as Jenna knew, he was an excellent friend. The best. One of her two pseudo-brothers with whom she'd sworn a blood oath the summer after sixth grade, almost twenty years ago.

From Jenna's perspective, Reece was at least as good as Brent, even if the latter scored bonus points because he was picking Jenna up at the airport while Reece was trying to fuck his personal demons into oblivion. Trying anything, in fact, that would exorcise the memory of how she'd clung to him that night, her curves enticing and her breath intoxicating, and not just because of the scent of too much alcohol.

She'd trusted him to be the white knight, her noble rescuer, and all he'd been able to think about was the feel of her body, soft and warm against his, as he carried her up the stairs to her apartment.

A wild craving had hit him that night, like a tidal wave of emotion crashing over him, washing away the outer shell of friendship and leaving nothing but raw desire and a longing so potent it nearly brought him to his knees.

It had taken all his strength to keep his distance when the only thing he'd wanted was to cover every inch of her naked body with kisses. To stroke her skin and watch her writhe with pleasure.

He'd won a hard-fought battle when he reined in his desire that night. But his victory wasn't without its wounds. She'd pierced his heart when she'd drifted to sleep in his arms, whispering that she loved him—and he knew that she meant it only as a friend.

More than that, he knew that he was the biggest asshole to ever walk the earth.

Thankfully, Jenna remembered nothing of that night. The liquor had stolen her memories, leaving her with a monster hangover, and him with a Jenna-shaped hole in his heart.

"Well?" Megan pressed. "Are you going to tell me? Or do I have to guess?"

"I blew off a friend."

"Yeah? That probably won't score you points in the Friend of the Year competition, but it doesn't sound too dire. Unless you were the best man and blew off the wedding? Left someone stranded at the side of the road somewhere in West Texas? Or promised to feed their cat and totally forgot? Oh, God. Please tell me you didn't kill Fluffy."

He bit back a laugh, feeling slightly better. "A friend came in tonight, and I feel like a complete shit for not meeting her plane."

"Well, there are taxis. And I assume she's an adult?"

"She is, and another friend is there to pick her up."

"I see," she said, and the way she slowly nodded suggested that she saw too much. "I'm guessing that *friend* means *girlfriend*? Or, no. You wouldn't do that. So she must be an ex."

"Really not," he assured her. "Just a friend. Life-long, since sixth grade."

"Oh, I get it. Longtime friend. High expecta-tions. She's going to be pissed."

"Nah. She's cool. Besides, she knows I usually work nights."

"Then what's the problem?"

He ran his hand over his shaved head, the bristles from the day's growth like sandpaper against his palm. "Hell if I know," he lied, then forced a smile, because whether his problem was guilt or lust or just plain stupidity, she hardly deserved to be on the receiving end of his bullshit.

He rattled his car keys. "How about I buy you one last drink before I take you home?"

"You're sure you don't mind a working drink?" Reece asked as he helped Megan out of his cherished baby blue vintage Chevy pickup. "Normally I wouldn't take you to my job, but we just hired a new bar back, and I want to see how it's going."

He'd snagged one of the coveted parking spots on Sixth Street, about a block down from The Fix, and he glanced automatically toward the bar, the glow from the windows relaxing him. He didn't own the place, but it was like a second home to him and had been for one hell of a long time.

"There's a new guy in training, and you're not there? I thought you told me you were the manager?"

"I did, and I am, but Tyree's there. The owner, I mean. He's always on site when someone new is starting. Says it's his job, not mine. Besides, Sunday's my day off, and Tyree's a stickler for keeping to the schedule."

"Okay, but why are you going then?"

"Honestly? The new guy's my cousin. He'll probably give me shit for checking in on him, but old habits die hard." Michael had been almost four when Vincent died, and the loss of his dad hit him hard. At sixteen, Reece had tried to be stoic, but Uncle Vincent had been like a second father to him, and he'd always thought of Mike as more brother than cousin. Either way, from that day on, he'd made it his job to watch out for the kid.

"Nah, he'll appreciate it," Megan said. "I've got a little sister, and she gripes when I check up on her, but it's all for show. She likes knowing I have her back. And as for getting a drink where you work, I don't mind at all."

As a general rule, late nights on Sunday were dead, both in the bar and on Sixth Street, the popular downtown Austin street that had been a focal point of the city's nightlife for decades. Tonight was no exception. At half-past one in the morning, the street was mostly deserted. Just a few cars moving slowly, their headlights shining toward the west, and a smattering of couples, stumbling and laughing. Probably tourists on their way back to one of the downtown hotels.

It was late April, though, and the spring weather was drawing both locals and tourists. Soon, the area—and the bar—would be bursting at the seams. Even on a slow Sunday night.

Situated just a few blocks down from Congress Avenue, the main downtown artery, The Fix on Sixth attracted a healthy mix of tourists and locals. The bar had existed in one form or another for decades, becoming a local staple, albeit one that had been falling deeper and deeper into disrepair until Tyree had bought the place six years ago and started it on much-needed life support.

"You've never been here before?" Reece asked as he paused in front of the oak and glass doors etched with the bar's familiar logo.

"I only moved downtown last month. I was in Los Angeles before."

The words hit Reece with unexpected force. Jenna had been in LA, and a wave of both longing and regret crashed over him. He should have gone with Brent. What the hell kind of friend was he, punishing Jenna because he couldn't control his own damn libido?

With effort, he forced the thoughts back. He'd

already beaten that horse to death.

"Come on," he said, sliding one arm around her shoulder and pulling open the door with his other. "You're going to love it."

He led her inside, breathing in the familiar mix of alcohol, southern cooking, and something indiscernible he liked to think of as the scent of a damn good time. As he expected, the place was mostly empty. There was no live music on Sunday nights, and at less than an hour to closing, there were only three customers in the front room.

"Megan, meet Cameron," Reece said, pulling out a stool for her as he nodded to the bartender in introduction. Down the bar, he saw Griffin Draper, a regular, lift his head, his face obscured by his hoodie, but his attention on Megan as she chatted with Cam about the house wines.

Reece nodded hello, but Griffin turned back to his notebook so smoothly and nonchalantly that Reece wondered if maybe he'd just been staring into space, thinking, and hadn't seen Reece or Megan at all. That was probably the case, actually. Griff wrote a popular podcast that had been turned into an even more popular web series, and when he wasn't recording the dialogue, he was usually writing a script.

"So where's Mike? With Tyree?"

Cameron made a face, looking younger than his twenty-four years. "Tyree's gone."

"You're kidding. Did something happen with Mike?" His cousin was a responsible kid. Surely he hadn't somehow screwed up his first day on the job.

"No, Mike's great." Cam slid a Scotch in front of Reece. "Sharp, quick, hard worker. He went off the clock about an hour ago, though. So you just missed him."

"Tyree shortened his shift?"

Cam shrugged. "Guess so. Was he supposed to be on until closing?"

"Yeah." Reece frowned. "He was. Tyree say why he cut him loose?"

"No, but don't sweat it. Your cousin's fitting right in. Probably just because it's Sunday and slow. " He made a face. "And since Tyree followed him out, guess who's closing for the first time alone."

"So you're in the hot seat, huh? " Reece tried to sound casual. He was standing behind Megan's stool, but now he moved to lean against the bar, hoping his casual posture suggested that he wasn't worried at all. He was, but he didn't want Cam to realize it. Tyree didn't leave employees to close on their own. Not until he'd spent weeks training them.

"I told him I want the weekend assistant manager position. I'm guessing this is his way of seeing how I work under pressure."

"Probably," Reece agreed half-heartedly. "What did he say?"

"Honestly, not much. He took a call in the office, told Mike he could head home, then about fifteen minutes later said he needed to take off, too, and that I was the man for the night."

"Trouble?" Megan asked.

"No. Just chatting up my boy," Reece said, surprised at how casual his voice sounded. Because the scenario had trouble printed all over it. He just wasn't sure what kind of trouble.

He focused again on Cam. "What about the waitstaff?" Normally, Tiffany would be in the main bar taking care of the customers who sat at tables. "He didn't send them home, too, did he?"

"Oh, no," Cam said. "Tiffany and Aly are scheduled to be on until closing, and they're in the back with—"

But his last words were drowned out by a high-pitched squeal of "*You're here!*" and Reece looked up to find Jenna Montgomery—the woman he craved —barreling across the room and flinging herself into his arms.

Meet Damien Stark

Only his passion could set her free…

Release Me
Claim Me
Complete Me
Anchor Me
Lost With Me

Meet Damien Stark in Release Me, *book 1 of the wildly sensual series that's left millions of readers breathless …*

Chapter One

A cool ocean breeze caresses my bare shoulders, and I shiver, wishing I'd taken my roommate's advice and brought a shawl with me tonight. I arrived in Los Angeles only four days ago, and I haven't yet adjusted to the concept of summer temperatures changing with the setting of the sun. In Dallas, June is hot, July is hotter, and August is hell.

Not so in California, at least not by the beach. LA Lesson Number One: Always carry a sweater if you'll be out after dark.

Of course, I could leave the balcony and go back inside to the party. Mingle with the million-aires. Chat up the celebrities. Gaze dutifully at the paintings. It is a gala art opening, after all, and my boss brought me here to meet and greet and charm and chat. Not to lust over the panorama that is coming alive in front of me. Bloodred clouds bursting against the pale orange sky. Blue-gray waves shimmering with dappled gold.

I press my hands against the balcony rail and lean forward, drawn to the intense, unreachable beauty of the setting sun. I regret that I didn't bring the battered Nikon I've had since high school. Not that it would have fit in my itty-bitty beaded purse. And a bulky camera bag paired with a little black dress is a big, fat fashion no-no.

But this is my very first Pacific Ocean sunset,

and I'm determined to document the moment. I pull out my iPhone and snap a picture.

"Almost makes the paintings inside seem redundant, doesn't it?" I recognize the throaty, feminine voice and turn to face Evelyn Dodge, retired actress turned agent turned patron of the arts—and my hostess for the evening.

"I'm so sorry. I know I must look like a giddy tourist, but we don't have sunsets like this in Dallas."

"Don't apologize," she says. "I pay for that view every month when I write the mortgage check. It damn well better be spectacular."

I laugh, immediately more at ease.

"Hiding out?"

"Excuse me?"

"You're Carl's new assistant, right?" she asks, referring to my boss of three days.

"Nikki Fairchild."

"I remember now. Nikki from Texas." She looks me up and down, and I wonder if she's disappointed that I don't have big hair and cowboy boots. "So who does he want you to charm?"

"Charm?" I repeat, as if I don't know exactly what she means.

She cocks a single brow. "Honey, the man would

rather walk on burning coals than come to an art show. He's fishing for investors and you're the bait." She makes a rough noise in the back of her throat. "Don't worry. I won't press you to tell me who. And I don't blame you for hiding out. Carl's brilliant, but he's a bit of a prick."

"It's the brilliant part I signed on for," I say, and she barks out a laugh.

The truth is that she's right about me being the bait. "Wear a cocktail dress," Carl had said. "Something flirty."

Seriously? I mean, *Seriously?*

I should have told him to wear his own damn cocktail dress. But I didn't. Because I want this job. I fought to get this job. Carl's company, C-Squared Technologies, successfully launched three web-based products in the last eighteen months. That track record had caught the industry's eye, and Carl had been hailed as a man to watch.

More important from my perspective, that meant he was a man to learn from, and I'd prepared for the job interview with an intensity bordering on obsession. Landing the position had been a huge coup for me. So what if he wanted me to wear something flirty? It was a small price to pay.

Shit.

"I need to get back to being the bait," I say.

"Oh, hell. Now I've gone and made you feel either guilty or self-conscious. Don't be. Let them get liquored up in there first. You catch more flies with alcohol anyway. Trust me. I know."

She's holding a pack of cigarettes, and now she taps one out, then extends the pack to me. I shake my head. I love the smell of tobacco—it reminds me of my grandfather—but actually inhaling the smoke does nothing for me.

"I'm too old and set in my ways to quit," she says. "But God forbid I smoke in my own damn house. I swear, the mob would burn me in effigy. You're not going to start lecturing me on the dangers of secondhand smoke, are you?"

"No," I promise.

"Then how about a light?"

I hold up the itty-bitty purse. "One lipstick, a credit card, my driver's license, and my phone."

"No condom?"

"I didn't think it was that kind of party," I say dryly.

"I knew I liked you." She glances around the balcony. "What the hell kind of party am I throwing if I don't even have one goddamn candle on one goddamn table? Well, fuck it." She puts the unlit cigarette to her mouth and inhales, her eyes closed and her expression rapturous. I can't help but like her. She wears hardly any makeup, in stark contrast to all the other women here tonight, myself included, and her dress is more of a caftan, the batik pattern as interesting as the woman herself.

She's what my mother would call a brassy broad —loud, large, opinionated, and self-confident. My mother would hate her. I think she's awesome.

She drops the unlit cigarette onto the tile and grinds it with the toe of her shoe. Then she signals to one of the catering staff, a girl dressed all in black and carrying a tray of champagne glasses.

The girl fumbles for a minute with the sliding door that opens onto the balcony, and I imagine those flutes tumbling off, breaking against the hard tile, the scattered shards glittering like a wash of diamonds.

I picture myself bending to snatch up a broken stem. I see the raw edge cutting into the soft flesh at the base of my thumb as I squeeze. I watch myself clutching it tighter, drawing strength from the pain, the way some people might try to extract luck from a rabbit's foot.

The fantasy blurs with memory, jarring me with its potency. It's fast and powerful, and a little disturbing because I haven't needed the pain in a long time, and I don't understand why I'm thinking about it now, when I feel steady and in control.

I am fine, I think. *I am fine, I am fine, I am fine.*

"Take one, honey," Evelyn says easily, holding a flute out to me.

I hesitate, searching her face for signs that my mask has slipped and she's caught a glimpse of my rawness. But her face is clear and genial.

"No, don't you argue," she adds, misinterpreting my hesitation. "I bought a dozen cases and I hate to see good alcohol go to waste. Hell no," she adds when the girl tries to hand her a flute. "I hate the stuff. Get me a vodka. Straight up. Chilled. Four olives. Hurry up, now. Do you want me to dry up like a leaf and float away?"

The girl shakes her head, looking a bit like a twitchy, frightened rabbit. Possibly one that had sacrificed his foot for someone else's good luck.

Evelyn's attention returns to me. "So how do you like LA? What have you seen? Where have you been? Have you bought a map of the stars yet? Dear God, tell me you're not getting sucked into all that tourist bullshit."

"Mostly I've seen miles of freeway and the inside of my apartment."

"Well, that's just sad. Makes me even more glad that Carl dragged your skinny ass all the way out here tonight."

I've put on fifteen welcome pounds since the years when my mother monitored every tiny thing that went in my mouth, and while I'm perfectly happy with my size-eight ass, I wouldn't describe it as skinny. I know Evelyn means it as a compliment, though, and so I smile. "I'm glad he brought me, too. The paintings really are amazing."

"Now don't do that—don't you go sliding into the polite-conversation routine. No, no," she says before I can protest. "I'm sure you mean it. Hell, the paintings are wonderful. But you're getting the flat-eyed look of a girl on her best behavior, and we can't have that. Not when I was getting to know the real you."

"Sorry," I say. "I swear I'm not fading away on you."

Because I genuinely like her, I don't tell her that she's wrong—she hasn't met the real Nikki Fairchild. She's met Social Nikki who, much like Malibu Barbie, comes with a complete set of accessories. In my case, it's not a bikini and a convertible. Instead, I have the *Elizabeth Fairchild Guide for Social Gatherings*.

My mother's big on rules. She claims it's her Southern upbringing. In my weaker moments, I agree. Mostly, I just think she's a controlling bitch. Since the first time she took me for tea at the Mansion at Turtle Creek in Dallas at age three, I have had the rules drilled into my head. How to walk, how to talk, how to dress. What to eat, how much to drink, what kinds of jokes to tell.

I have it all down, every trick, every nuance, and I wear my practiced pageant smile like armor against the world. The result being that I don't think I could truly be myself at a party even if my life depended on it.

This, however, is not something Evelyn needs to know.

"Where exactly are you living?" she asks.

"Studio City. I'm sharing a condo with my best friend from high school."

"Straight down the 101 for work and then back home again. No wonder you've only seen concrete. Didn't anyone tell you that you should have taken an apartment on the Westside?"

"Too pricey to go it alone," I admit, and I can tell that my admission surprises her. When I make the effort—like when I'm Social Nikki—I can't help but look like I come from money. Probably because

I do. Come from it, that is. But that doesn't mean I brought it with me.

"How old are you?"

"Twenty-four."

Evelyn nods sagely, as if my age reveals some secret about me. "You'll be wanting a place of your own soon enough. You call me when you do and we'll find you someplace with a view. Not as good as this one, of course, but we can manage something better than a freeway on-ramp."

"It's not that bad, I promise."

"Of course it's not," she says in a tone that says the exact opposite. "As for views," she continues, gesturing toward the now-dark ocean and the sky that's starting to bloom with stars, "you're welcome to come back anytime and share mine."

"I might take you up on that," I admit. "I'd love to bring a decent camera back here and take a shot or two."

"It's an open invitation. I'll provide the wine and you can provide the entertainment. A young woman loose in the city. Will it be a drama? A rom-com? Not a tragedy, I hope. I love a good cry as much as the next woman, but I like you. You need a happy ending."

I tense, but Evelyn doesn't know she's hit a

nerve. That's why I moved to LA, after all. New life. New story. New Nikki.

I ramp up the Social Nikki smile and lift my champagne flute. "To happy endings. And to this amazing party. I think I've kept you from it long enough."

"Bullshit," she says. "I'm the one monopolizing you, and we both know it."

We slip back inside, the buzz of alcohol-fueled conversation replacing the soft calm of the ocean.

"The truth is, I'm a terrible hostess. I do what I want, talk to whoever I want, and if my guests feel slighted they can damn well deal with it."

I gape. I can almost hear my mother's cries of horror all the way from Dallas.

"Besides," she continues, "this party isn't supposed to be about me. I put together this little shindig to introduce Blaine and his art to the community. He's the one who should be doing the mingling, not me. I may be fucking him, but I'm not going to baby him."

Evelyn has completely destroyed my image of how a hostess for the not-to-be-missed social event of the weekend is supposed to behave, and I think I'm a little in love with her for that.

"I haven't met Blaine yet. That's him, right?" I

point to a tall reed of a man. He is bald, but sports a red goatee. I'm pretty sure it's not his natural color. A small crowd hums around him, like bees drawing nectar from a flower. His outfit is certainly as bright as one.

"That's my little center of attention, all right," Evelyn says. "The man of the hour. Talented, isn't he?" Her hand sweeps out to indicate her massive living room. Every wall is covered with paintings. Except for a few benches, whatever furniture was once in the room has been removed and replaced with easels on which more paintings stand.

I suppose technically they are portraits. The models are nudes, but these aren't like anything you would see in a classical art book. There's something edgy about them. Something provocative and raw. I can tell that they are expertly conceived and carried out, and yet they disturb me, as if they reveal more about the person viewing the portrait than about the painter or the model.

As far as I can tell, I'm the only one with that reaction. Certainly the crowd around Blaine is glowing. I can hear the gushing praise from here.

"I picked a winner with that one," Evelyn says. "But let's see. Who do you want to meet? Rip Carrington and Lyle Tarpin? Those two are guaranteed drama, that's for damn sure, and your room-mate will be jealous as hell if you chat them up."

"She will?"

Evelyn's brows arch up. "Rip and Lyle? They've been feuding for weeks." She narrows her eyes at me. "The fiasco about the new season of their sitcom? It's all over the Internet? You really don't know them?"

"Sorry," I say, feeling the need to apologize. "My school schedule was pretty intense. And I'm sure you can imagine what working for Carl is like."

Speaking of …

I glance around, but I don't see my boss anywhere.

"That is one serious gap in your education," Evelyn says. "Culture—and yes, pop culture counts —is just as important as—what did you say you studied?"

"I don't think I mentioned it. But I have a double major in electrical engineering and computer science."

"So you've got brains and beauty. See? That's something else we have in common. Gotta say, though, with an education like that, I don't see why you signed up to be Carl's secretary."

I laugh. "I'm not, I swear. Carl was looking for

someone with tech experience to work with him on the business side of things, and I was looking for a job where I could learn the business side. Get my feet wet. I think he was a little hesitant to hire me at first—my skills definitely lean toward tech—but I convinced him I'm a fast learner."

She peers at me. "I smell ambition."

I lift a shoulder in a casual shrug. "It's Los Angeles. Isn't that what this town is all about?"

"Ha! Carl's lucky he's got you. It'll be interesting to see how long he keeps you. But let's see … who here would intrigue you …?"

She casts about the room, finally pointing to a fifty-something man holding court in a corner. "That's Charles Maynard," she says. "I've known Charlie for years. Intimidating as hell until you get to know him. But it's worth it. His clients are either celebrities with name recognition or power brokers with more money than God. Either way, he's got all the best stories."

"He's a lawyer?"

"With Bender, Twain & McGuire. Very prestigious firm."

"I know," I say, happy to show that I'm not entirely ignorant, despite not knowing Rip or Lyle. "One of my closest friends works for the firm. He started here but he's in their New York office now."

"Well, come on, then, Texas. I'll introduce you." We take one step in that direction, but then Evelyn stops me. Maynard has pulled out his phone, and is shouting instructions at someone. I catch a few well-placed curses and eye Evelyn sideways. She looks unconcerned "He's a pussycat at heart. Trust me, I've worked with him before. Back in my agenting days, we put together more celebrity biopic deals for our clients than I can count. And we fought to keep a few tell-alls off the screen, too." She shakes her head, as if reliving those glory days, then pats my arm. "Still, we'll wait 'til he calms down a bit. In the meantime, though …"

She trails off, and the corners of her mouth turn down in a frown as she scans the room again. "I don't think he's here yet, but—oh! Yes! Now *there's* someone you should meet. And if you want to talk views, the house he's building has one that makes my view look like, well, like yours." She points toward the entrance hall, but all I see are bobbing heads and haute couture. "He hardly ever accepts invitations, but we go way back," she says.

I still can't see who she's talking about, but then the crowd parts and I see the man in profile. Goose bumps rise on my arms, but I'm not cold. In fact, I'm suddenly very, very warm.

He's tall and so handsome that the word is almost an insult. But it's more than that. It's not his looks, it's his *presence*. He commands the room simply by being in it, and I realize that Evelyn and I aren't the only ones looking at him. The entire crowd has noticed his arrival. He must feel the weight of all those eyes, and yet the attention doesn't faze him at all. He smiles at the girl with the champagne, takes a glass, and begins to chat casually with a woman who approaches him, a simpering smile stretched across her face.

"Damn that girl," Evelyn says. "She never did bring me my vodka."

But I barely hear her. "Damien Stark," I say. My voice surprises me. It's little more than breath.

Evelyn's brows rise so high I notice the movement in my peripheral vision. "Well, how about that?" she says knowingly. "Looks like I guessed right."

"You did," I admit. "Mr. Stark is just the man I want to see."

I hope you enjoyed the excerpt! Grab your own copy of Release Me ... or any of the books in the series now!

The Original Trilogy

Release Me

Claim Me

Complete Me

And Beyond...

Anchor Me

Lost With Me

Some rave reviews for J. Kenner's sizzling romances...

I just get sucked into these books and can not get enough of this series. They are so well written and as satisfying as each book is they leave you greedy for more. — Goodreads reviewer on *Wicked Torture*

A sizzling, intoxicating, sexy read!!!! J. Kenner had me devouring Wicked Dirty, the second installment of *Stark World Series* in one sitting. I loved everything about this book from the opening pages to the raw and vulnerable characters. With her sophisticated prose, Kenner created a love story that had the perfect blend of lust, passion, sexual tension, raw emotions and love. - Michelle, Four Chicks Flipping Pages

Wicked Dirty CLAIMED and CONSUMED every ounce of me from the very first page. Mind racing. Pulse pounding. Breaths bated. Feels flowing. Eyes wide in anticipation. Heart beating out of my chest. I felt the current of *Wicked Dirty* flow through me. I was DRUNK on this book that was my fine whiskey, so smooth and spectacular, and could not get enough of this *Wicked Dirty* drink. - Karen Bookalicious Babes Blog

"Sinfully sexy and full of heart. Kenner shines in this second chance, slow burn of a romance. Wicked Grind is the perfect book to kick off your summer."- *K. Bromberg, New York Times bestselling author (on Wicked Grind)*

"J. Kenner never disappoints~her books just get better and better." - *Mom's Guilty Pleasure (on Wicked Grind)*

"I don't think J. Kenner could write a bad story if she tried. ... Wicked Grind is a great beginning to what I'm positive will be a very successful series. ... The line forms here." *iScream Books (On Wicked Grind)*

"Scorching, sweet, and soul-searing, *Anchor Me* is the ultimate love story that stands the test of time and tribulation. THE TRUEST LOVE!" *Bookalicious Babes Blog (on Anchor Me)*

"J. Kenner has brought this couple to life and the character connection that I have to these two holds no bounds and that is testament to J.

Kenner's writing ability." *The Romance Cover (on Anchor Me)*

"J. Kenner writes an emotional and personal story line. … The premise will captivate your imagination; the characters will break your heart; the romance continues to push the envelope." *The Reading Café (on Anchor Me)*

"Kenner may very well have cornered the market on sinfully attractive, dominant antiheroes and the women who swoon for them . . ." *Romantic Times*

"*Wanted* is another J. Kenner masterpiece . . . This was an intriguing look at self-discovery and forbidden love all wrapped into a neat little action-suspense package. There was plenty of sexual tension and eventually action. Evan was hot, hot, hot! Together, they were combustible. But can we expect anything less from J. Kenner?" *Reading Haven*

"*Wanted* by J. Kenner is the whole package! A toe-curling smokin' hot read, full of incredible characters and a brilliant storyline that you won't be able to get enough of. I can't wait for the next book in this series . . . I'm hooked!" *Flirty & Dirty Book Blog*

"J. Kenner's evocative writing thrillingly captures the power of physical attraction, the pull of longing, the universe-altering effect one person can have on another. . . . *Claim Me* has the emotional depth to back up the sex . . . Every scene is infused with both erotic tension, and the tension of wondering what lies beneath Damien's veneer – and how and when it will be revealed." *Heroes and Heartbreakers*

"*Claim Me* by J. Kenner is an erotic, sexy and exciting ride. The story between Damien and Nikki is amazing and written beautifully. The intimate and detailed sex scenes will leave you fanning yourself to cool down. With the writing style of Ms. Kenner you almost feel like you are there in the story riding along the emotional rollercoaster with Damien and Nikki." *Fresh Fiction*

"PERFECT for fans of *Fifty Shades of Grey* and *Bared to You. Release Me* is a powerful and erotic romance novel that is sure to make adult romance readers sweat, sigh and swoon." *Reading, Eating & Dreaming Blog*

"I will admit, I am in the 'I loved *Fifty Shades*' camp,

but after reading *Release Me*, Mr. Grey only scratches the surface compared to Damien Stark." *Cocktails and Books Blog*

"It is not often when a book is so amazingly well-written that I find it hard to even begin to accurately describe it . . . I recommend this book to everyone who is interested in a passionate love story." *Romancebookworm's Reviews*

"The story is one that will rank up with the *Fifty Shades* and Cross Fire trilogies." *Incubus Publishing Blog*

"The plot is complex, the characters engaging, and J. Kenner's passionate writing brings it all perfectly together." *Harlequin Junkie*

Also by J. Kenner

The Stark Saga Novels:

Only his passion could set her free…

Meet Damien Stark

The Original Trilogy

Release Me

Claim Me

Complete Me

And Beyond…

Anchor Me

Lost With Me

Stark Ever After

(Stark Saga novellas):

Happily ever after is just the beginning.

The passion between Damien & Nikki continues.

Take Me

Have Me

Play My Game

Seduce Me

Unwrap Me

Deepest Kiss

Entice Me

Hold Me

Please Me

The Steele Books/Stark International:

He was the only man who made her feel alive.

Say My Name

On My Knees

Under My Skin

Take My Dare (includes short story Steal My Heart)

Stark International Novellas:

Meet Jamie & Ryan-so hot it sizzles.

Tame Me

Tempt Me

S.I.N. Trilogy:

It was wrong for them to be together…

…but harder to stay apart.

Dirtiest Secret

Hottest Mess

Sweetest Taboo

Stand alone novels:

Most Wanted:

Three powerful, dangerous men.

Three sensual, seductive women.

Wanted

Heated

Ignited

Wicked Nights (Stark World):

Sometimes it feels so damn good to be bad.

Wicked Grind

Wicked Dirty

Wicked Torture

Man of the Month

Who's your man of the month …?

Down On Me

Hold On Tight

Need You Now

Start Me Up

Get It On

In Your Eyes

Turn Me On

Shake It Up

All Night Long

In Too Deep

Light My Fire

Walk The Line

Bar Bites: A Man of the Month Cookbook(by J. Kenner
& Suzanne M. Johnson)

Additional Titles

Wild Thing

One Night (A Stark World short story in the Second
Chances anthology)

Also by Julie Kenner

The Protector (Superhero) Series:
The Cat's Fancy (prequel)
Aphrodite's Kiss
Aphrodite's Passion
Aphrodite's Secret
Aphrodite's Flame
Aphrodite's Embrace (novella)
Aphrodite's Delight (novella – free download)

Demon Hunting Soccer Mom Series:
Carpe Demon
California Demon
Demons Are Forever
Deja Demon
The Demon You Know (short story)
Demon Ex Machina

Also by Julie Kenner

Pax Demonica
Day of the Demon

The Dark Pleasures Series:
Caress of Darkness
Find Me In Darkness
Find Me In Pleasure
Find Me In Passion
Caress of Pleasure

The Blood Lily Chronicles:
Tainted
Torn
Turned

Rising Storm:
Rising Storm: Tempest Rising
Rising Storm: Quiet Storm

Devil May Care:
Seducing Sin
Tempting Fate

About the Author

J. Kenner (aka Julie Kenner) is the *New York Times*, *USA Today*, *Publishers Weekly*, *Wall Street Journal* and #1 International bestselling author of over eighty novels, novellas and short stories in a variety of genres.

JK has been praised by *Publishers Weekly* as an author with a "flair for dialogue and eccentric characterizations" and by *RT Bookclub* for having "cornered the market on sinfully attractive, dominant antiheroes and the women who swoon for them." A five-time finalist for Romance Writers of America's prestigious RITA award, JK took home the first RITA trophy awarded in the category of erotic romance in 2014 for her novel, *Claim Me* (book 2 of her Stark Trilogy).

In her previous career as an attorney, JK worked as a lawyer in Southern California and Texas. She currently lives in Central Texas, with her husband, two daughters, and two rather spastic cats.

More ways to connect:
www.jkenner.com
Text JKenner to 21000 for JK's text alerts.

facebook.com/jkennerbooks
twitter.com/juliekenner

CPSIA information can be obtained
at www.ICGtesting.com
Printed in the USA
LVHW041443161218
600666LV00018B/698/P

9 781940 673776